"He's playing  offered his advice right. But the p[u] problem right now. He still had his eyes shut and his jaw was clenched as tightly as the rest of his body, and Amy was pretty sure she had a good idea why.

From a distance, she heard the boys continue to give her advice, but she couldn't concentrate on what they were saying because she was too busy coming to grips with the realization that her hips were almost even with Nick's. With their bare bellies all but glued to one another, she had a firsthand feel of the steel button of his jeans pressing into her flesh. And that wasn't all that was pressing into her.

No, Nick definitely wasn't playing dead.

Her eyes widened in shock, just about the time he opened his. They stared at each other in uncomfortable silence. She had no idea how to make it stop, or if she even wanted to. The idea that she aroused Nick was so new and so amazing she didn't want to give it up yet, even though it almost killed her to hold his gaze while they each adjusted to this new reality.

"Are you going to finish me off?" Nick asked in a whisper, his eyes staring unflinchingly into hers.

"What?" Amy rasped. His voice was so low she wasn't sure what he'd said. She lowered her gaze to his lips in an attempt to read them when he repeated himself, but they didn't move. His mouth was inches away from hers and slowly her head started to lower. Her vision encompassed only her target and as her whole body relaxed into his, her hands released his, but he kept them planted on the floor where they were.

This was it. Do it or die, Amy. If you don't do it, you might just die without ever finding out.

"One, two, three," Jacob counted, jarring Amy's concentration. "Aunt Amy won!"

"*Ew*, they're gonna kiss," Kevin added his observations at almost the same time in a disgusted little boy tone.

Embrace the passion of Echelon Press

ATTENTION: ORGANIZATIONS AND CORPORATIONS
Most Echelon Press books are available for special discounting in bulk quantities for sales promotions and special events. For more information please visit **www.echelonpress.com**

Gerrie Shepard

Best Laid Plans

This is a work of fiction. Names, characters, places, and incidents are products of the author's imagination or are used fictitiously and are not to be construed as real. Any resemblance to actual events, locales, organizations, or persons, living or dead, is entirely coincidental.

Echelon Press
712 Briarwood Lane
Hurst, Texas

Copyright © 2004 by Gerrie Shepard
ISBN: 1-59080-214-4
www.echelonpress.com

All rights reserved. No part of this book may be used or reproduced in any manner whatsoever without written permission, except in the case of brief quotations embodied in critical articles and reviews. For information address Echelon Press.

First Echelon Press paperback printing: August 2004
Cover Art © Nathalie Moore

Embrace and all its logos are trademarks of Echelon Press.

Printed in Lavergne, TN, USA

Dear Readers,

Over the last year Echelon Press has been blessed with a number of wonderful changes. With the transition of management comes growth and progress.

Echelon Press , management and authors, are committed to offering you the most entertaining stories we can. With something for everything, from children to even the most seasoned reader, Echelon offers award winning books and award winning authors to ensure the highest possible quality of writing.

This month we offer you the debut novel from Gerrie Shepard, BEST LAID PLANS. Sometimes we just need to sit down and take time for ourselves. During that time a smile or a giggle can work wonders on the weary soul.

Gerrie Shepard offers plenty of both, with a healthy does of love to top it off. Hailing from down south in Florida, Ms. Shepard offers readers the warm and refreshing depth that makes romance one of the most widely read genres in fiction.

And don't forget, if it's adventure and thrills that get your adrenaline flowing, you can find the debut novel, THE LAST OPERATION from New Yorker, Patrick Astre.

Echelon Press is always pleased to hear your thoughts and suggestions for how we can make our publishing house, your publishing house! Please send your comments to suggestions@echelonpress.com.

Happy Reading!

Karen L. Syed, President
Echelon Press

Dedication

For Merry:
Sometimes we ran, sometimes we walked, and sometimes we just sat down in the dust and refused to budge.
Thanks for letting me sit, but not for too long.

Gerrie Shepard

Chapter One

Nick Granger leaned back in the canvas patio chair and smiled. Just a few days before Thanksgiving and here he was, lounging by the pool and contemplating his good fortune. All while waiting for the football game to start. Nothing could ruin this day.

Finally, his persistence had paid off. Every six months for the past ten years he'd submitted a resume to his favorite pro-football team's personnel department. He'd kept them updated on his skills, accomplishments, interests, and his repeated willingness to relocate from sunny Florida to a more seasonal clime.

In each of his numerous employment approaches he'd made it specifically clear he was willing to fulfill whatever position the management team felt he was most competent to handle.

With his background in physical therapy, surely they'd want him taking care of the players and working them through their injuries. All he needed was a chance to prove himself, become invaluable to the team, and he'd be in for good.

A grin curved his lips as he remembered telling his best friend, Ted, about the recent job offer. To say Ted was envious would be an understatement.

Oh, yes, Nick thought. It was good to be the physical therapist in charge of the team's cheerleaders.

At first he'd been bothered that someone had sent his

resume to the cheerleading office. He wanted to work with the players, not the pep squad. Then his optimism and enthusiasm overcame his affront and he decided to view it as an opportunity.

Granted, he wouldn't be working in the heart of pro-football, but he certainly could stand being in the bosom of the sport. He chuckled. Honestly, was there anyone luckier than he?

Still, he would miss Ted, and his wife and kids. Not to mention Amy, Ted's sister. The two of them were the only family Nick could or would claim since his mother had run off to join the circus, leaving him with his grandmother, Nellie. She'd done her best to raise him, bless her departed, blue-haired self, but a boy wants male companionship.

Until the day he met Ted Gilbert at Little League practice. Ted became his longed-for brother and his whole family took Nick in.

He sat now in the shadows of Ted's verandah, rocking his foot back and forth on a striped beach ball as he contemplated the next phase of his life.

Hearing splashing coming from the pool, he frowned, knowing Amy and her boyfriend, Michael, were the cause. The realization that he was literally the fifth wheel in this small get-together of couples hit him. It took him almost three seconds to remind himself he couldn't become involved right now. He was moving soon, for pity's sake.

Feeling a thump on the back of his head, he looked over his shoulder. "Hey, Buddy," he said.

Ted saluted him with his barbecue tongs. Wearing a camouflage print apron that proclaimed him as "Grill Sergeant," complete with a loop on the side for the tongs and pockets for spices, Ted was ready for an afternoon of barbecuing. "I'm fixin' to put the steaks on," he said. "You want yours raw, I mean, *rare*, right?"

Nick gave a mock shudder. "Burn it, my friend. Make it beg for mercy."

Ted tossed him a disgusted look. "Where's the challenge in that? Anyone can burn a steak. It takes real talent to get it just perfect."

"Burnt is just perfect," he insisted.

"Peasant," Ted shot over his shoulder as he stalked away, a plate of steaks in his hand and two multi-colored oven mitts poking out of his back pocket.

"Nice mittens, Ted," he couldn't help observing.

Ted turned. "Thanks. Janelle says they compliment the gray in my eyes." He batted his eyelashes.

"Really? Janelle said that? Did she happen to mention if they compliment the gray in your hair?"

Janelle was Ted's wife and together they had two boys, who were napping. Not that they'd sleep through the whole barbecue; even Nick wasn't that naïve. They were just gathering their energy to take over the house later.

Man, he loved those kids.

"No, she said my only *slightly* graying hair is accentuated by my naturally tan and athletic physique." Ted drew his attention back to the conversation as he struck a bodybuilder's pose, barely balancing the steaks. "Now leave me alone, would ya?" he said as he left. "I've got manly things to do."

Nick grinned. He and Ted were the same age. But where Ted had found his first gray hair two years ago, he hadn't gotten his yet. Not that he was checking. He just knew that when he got one, his best friend would be sure to announce it to the world.

The pungent smell of grilling steaks reached him, promising good things to those who wait. Leaning back, Nick studied the ceiling fan spinning slowly overhead, his thoughts turning lazy circles in accompaniment. A low growl interrupted the serenity. Placing a palm on his stomach, he frowned. He was starving, but decided to pass on getting a snack. Ted and Janelle were putting the finishing touches on dinner and the least he could do was wait politely.

Stretching his feet out in front, he looked over his bare toes into the swimming pool and frowned. There was Ted's sister, Amy, floating on her back while Michael held her up and whispered in her ear. The only things clearly visible were her nose, her toes, and her breasts.

Averting his eyes quickly, Nick focused on Michael's encroaching presence. The frown became a scowl.

It wasn't that Nick disliked Michael. Not really. He was a great guy. It's just that he was so…blonde. Everything about him was blonde, from the hair on his head to the hair on his arms and legs. Even his eyebrows were blonde, for pity's sake. Not a white Nordic blonde, but rather a weathered, sun-streaked blonde. He had that "surfer" look about him. How did someone so blonde tan that dark anyway?

Amy suddenly bolted upright in the pool, swinging dripping hair out of her eyes as she turned and grabbed Michael's shoulders, her laugh as bright as the day. Nick sat up straight, just in time to see the other man grab Amy's waist and pull her in for a wet kiss.

Nick tightened his hands into fists before forcing them to relax. Reaching down, he grabbed the beach ball and taking careful aim, threw it at Michael.

But the pair shifted around at the last second so that Amy's back was facing Nick and the ball bounced off her shoulder.

"Hey," she shrieked, turning to face her attacker and squinting in the bright sun. The shadowy verandah and potted palms offered him some obscurity, but not much. She spotted him quick enough. "What was that for?"

"Let's keep in mind this is a family pool, and there are small children around." He leaned back against the chair again, his mission completed.

"I thought the kids were taking naps." Michael raised one blonde eyebrow.

Damn, he really wished he'd beaned Michael with that ball instead of Amy. "Oh, yeah," Nick said. "I forgot." He grinned without apology.

Amy made her way to the steps and climbed out of the pool, water streaming off her as she walked toward him. Michael followed close behind. Too close.

Grabbing a towel, she sauntered over to Nick's table. "That's cuz you're getting old and senile." She rubbed her hair in the terry towel, her arms strong and sure. "After all, the big three-*o* does that to a person."

She didn't look at him; too busy running the towel briskly over her body, catching every drop on its downward plunge. One droplet running slowly from her throat to her cleavage caught his attention.

As she used the towel to mop it up, he snapped his gaze to her face. She stared at him expectantly, waiting.

What had he missed? He looked at Michael. No help there, he was toweling off and looking at him too.

Nick replayed the last few seconds of conversation. He remembered her gibe about his age and grinned. This familiar territory Nick was comfortable with. "I wouldn't be throwing insults around, little girl. You'll be joining me in my dotage in three short years. Besides," he continued. "Thirty isn't old."

She rolled her eyes. "Yeah, if you're a tree." She slung her towel over the back of another patio chair. It hit with a smack. Hands on hips, she leaned toward him and said, "And in the three whole years before I turn thirty, you will become even more decrepit, Nicholas Granger, Forest Ranger."

Oh, she was going for the hardcore stuff, was she? He remembered the childhood name with embarrassment and she knew it, the insufferable brat. There was a time, before football, when he'd wanted to be a park ranger. Until he'd fallen out of a tree and broken his arm. Well, not exactly fallen, he recalled.

After that, it just didn't seem such a desirable vocation to the teenaged Nick. In fact, that experience fueled his interest in physical therapy. However, it had galled his adolescent pride that his friend's little pest of a sister had witnessed the whole thing.

"What do you have to say to that, Ranger Nick?" she continued, flipping her still wet hair behind a bare shoulder. He opened his mouth to speak just as Michael put his long, tanned arm around Amy's shoulders, his big hand dangling around her right breast.

Shock sizzled through his brain and fused his attention to the sight, making it impossible for him to look away. Not until he noticed a faint outline in the front of her bright yellow bathing suit top.

He blinked. Then stared harder. Sure enough, it was still there. The dark circle of Amy's nipple was clearly visible, even in the shadowed light of the verandah.

His pulse pounded in his ears, crushing his mood and blowing his perfect day all to hell.

Nick jumped up, his chair skidding out from behind him before finally tipping over onto its side. Stripping his T-shirt over his head, Nick threw it to Amy. "Maybe you should put some clothes on."

She caught the shirt without even looking at it and gaped at him, her face reddened either by the sun or embarrassment, he wasn't sure which.

Maybe it was the red haze hovering over his vision. Whatever it was, Nick was floundering in the aftermath of a careless act. That it was his second one today wasn't lost on him.

What's wrong with me?

He had the sinking suspicion he should apologize, but he wasn't quite sure why. He wasn't the one standing around half-naked in front of God and everyone.

He looked down. Actually, since he'd given her his shirt, he was standing around half-naked in front of God and everyone. But that was different.

"Hey, Nick," came a voice from the doorway. "Why don't you come help me in the kitchen? I need someone to chop the lettuce and you look like you need to cut something into pieces."

"Sure, Janelle." He bent to pick up the chair and pushed it under the table. He started to explain himself, but turned instead toward the kitchen door when no explanation occurred to him.

"What's up with him?" he heard Amy ask as he walked away.

"He's obviously not getting enough," Michael answered.

She laughed. "That's what you say about everything!"

"It's a guy thing," Michael reasoned. "But, I'm usually right."

Nick gritted his teeth and kept walking, admitting to himself that Michael was right. He'd have to do something about that. Soon.

8

Entering the kitchen, his bare feet padded softly on the white ceramic tile. Compared to the verandah's shady coolness, the kitchen was bright and warm, even though the windows over the sink were open. Wallpaper border with crowing roosters and nesting hens marched around the room's walls. Ceramic pigs and cows made themselves useful as spoon rests, butter dishes, and a bunch of other stuff he wasn't sure he could name, much less put to use if he had to.

Through the arched doorway into the formal dining room he noticed the preparations Janelle had made for a buffet-style lunch. Just beyond the potted palms framing the dining room's other entrance was the front door. He wondered fleetingly if he could make it out without her noticing.

No such luck. Glancing over at Janelle, she pointed him to a cutting board and a head of lettuce. A sharp knife lay on its side next to them. She raised her eyebrows and nodded toward the chore she'd assigned him, her black, hip-length braid swishing gently behind her as she went back to rinsing tomatoes at the sink.

Tucking himself up against the butcher-block countertop he set to work, concentrating hard on what he was doing.

Chop, chop, chop.

"Nick," Janelle said, grabbing his arm. "We want salad, not coleslaw."

He looked down. He'd started out fine, but the rhythmic, mindless chore had let his thoughts wander, and now he had a huge pile of slivered lettuce.

"Sorry," he said, scraping the whole mess off the giant-sized cutting board and into a large salad bowl. "I guess my mind was somewhere else. You want me to cut up some tomatoes?" he offered.

"Heck, no." She took the knife away from him. "I want you to tell me what that was all about outside."

Her brown eyes stared him down and Nick imagined he had a pretty good idea how her fourth grade students must feel when they didn't have their homework done. "You mean just now?"

"No, I mean last Christmas. Of course I mean now."

Standing there in front of him, wearing only a bathing suit and a flimsy little skirt tied around her hips she didn't appear too intimidating. However, since she had a sharp knife in her hand Nick figured he'd better answer.

"Oh, that." He wiped his hands on a towel, running the material over each finger individually, hoping Janelle would think of something vital she had to do. It wasn't happening.

Balling the towel up, he shot it into the sink, basketball style. He shrugged. "It's just Amy's bathing suit top is see-through, and I guess I got a little over-protective."

"Of what?" she wanted to know.

He didn't have an answer because he definitely hadn't done his homework on this one.

"Nick, she's an adult, has been for some time now. She can take care of herself, and if that means being with Michael, or anyone else for that matter, you're going to have to learn to deal with it. Or do something about it."

Before he could ask what that meant, Janelle set the knife down and crossed her arms over her bare midriff. "Besides," she said gently. "Her bathing suit is not see-through, Nick."

"What are you talking about? Of course it is, I saw it with my own eyes." He leaned back against the counter and stared at his bare toes, not exactly comfortable with where the conversation was headed. Looking at his feet against the stark, white tile it occurred to him that surfer dude Michael wasn't the only one with a tan.

"And what exactly did you see?" she demanded.

No way was he answering that. He already felt like a peeping Tom. She could put him in time-out forever and he'd still keep it to himself.

Janelle sighed. "She has the same bathing suit on that I do, it's just a different color." Holding her arms out away from her sides she asked, "Is my top see-through?"

Certain he was being punished for some heinous thing he'd done in a previous life, Nick stole a quick, embarrassed look. She was right. Damn.

He turned his gaze to stare at an old fashioned, white milk jug holding a variety of spatulas and spoons, its sides painted with big black splotches. He was almost positive it was supposed to be some sort of cow pun in ceramic.

He snapped his fingers and looked up. "Yeah, but hers was wet." He had her there.

"So is mine. Didn't I just get out of the pool a couple of minutes ago?" Standing there with her arms folded again, Nick decided she looked just like the teacher she was.

Well, hell. He couldn't argue with that. "Then it must be the light. Out there in the shadow it was more obvious, or something."

Janelle shook her head and grabbed a tomato. "Nick, honey, it'll take more than a change of light for you to see the obvious." She turned away to cut the tomato into neat slices.

What the hell was that suppose to mean? Too afraid to find out, he picked up a plastic tumbler and poured himself a glass of grape *Kool-Aid*. "Does this have half the sugar?"

"Yes," she answered. "Just like you like it."

"Thanks." He put the pitcher down and opened the freezer

door.

"Why don't you go help Ted with the steaks?" Janelle tossed over her shoulder as he filled his glass with ice. "Keep him out of trouble."

Yeah, that was likely to happen. The way his day was going, he'd probably end up getting Ted arrested on charges of impersonating a military chef or something.

Smiling at the thought of Ted doing time for felonious food preparation, he headed out the door.

Chapter Two

Amy spread a towel out on the chair and sat down, immediately reaching behind her to scratch a mosquito bite right in the middle of her back. Unable to reach it she leaned back and rubbed against the chair. Shimmying her shoulders back and forth for maximum scratchability, she stopped suddenly when she saw Nick watching her from the kitchen door.

Offering him a smile, she was about to invite him to join Michael and her when he shut the door and took off like someone had set his tail on fire.

It doesn't matter, she told herself. He was always running from her like she had the plague or something, ever since they were kids. Oh, she knew he liked her, probably even loved her in a sisterly way. He just didn't want to be around her for too long, and definitely not alone. In fact, if gossip around town didn't say differently, she'd think Nick didn't like women. That would be a real pity. Even if it would make her feel better to think it wasn't her he wasn't attracted to, but all women in general.

As Michael set up the game of checkers he'd found in the antique, pine cupboard against the wall, she wrinkled her brow in concern over Nick's behavior, which, if she was honest with herself, was getting worse the older they got. His jumpiness made her wish things could be different. Made her wish she wasn't his best friend's sister, or that she hadn't known him practically all her life.

"Hey, Ames," Michael said, interrupting her melancholy thoughts. "Just to make it interesting, let's play strip checkers."

So attuned to Nick's progress was she that she alone noticed the little stutter in his step, the stiffening in his spine. In response to Michael's suggestion?

No, that couldn't be it, she decided, turning her attention back to Michael. "Well, that wouldn't be fair." She looked him up and down. "Considering your bathing suit has only one piece, while mine has two."

Michael winked at her. "Good point. Take off your top."

Choking sounds coming from the other side of the pool drowned her laugh out. She looked up in time to see Nick bent over with Ted pounding on his back, the colorful oven mitt muffling the thumping noises, while a plastic cup rolled around on the ground in a purple puddle.

Amy rose, only to be restrained by Michael's hand. "He's a big boy, Amy. He'll be okay." Setting the last checker in place, he leaned back and crossed his arms. "Why are you always hovering over him? Is there something going on between the two of you I should know about?"

She dropped her mouth open in shock. "Why would you say that?" The question came out of the blue, pinpointing a secret Amy thought nobody knew.

"No reason, really. It just seems like whenever he's around you're always watching him and looking for reasons to be where he is."

Was that true?

Even before Michael finished speaking, Nick straightened. Staring over at her, he frowned, waving Ted off and trying to catch his breath.

What'd I do? She shrugged in response to his frown and turned her focus forcibly back to the checkers game that Michael had started without her. "You're imagining things," she reassured him. "And just to show you that you have my undivided attention, I'm going to whip your butt in checkers."

Thank goodness for Michael's competitive nature, she thought, as she moved her game piece. His focus was successfully diverted.

Strip checkers indeed. Apparently Nick thought the idea was as outrageous as she did. There was something sad about that.

* * *

Nick hit the button that controlled the sedan's sunroof as Amy climbed into the seat next to him. Hearing the *thwump* of the new car door shutting, he put the vehicle in reverse and used the rearview mirror to back out of Ted's and Janelle's driveway, then drove down the quiet street.

He loved this car. It was the first brand new vehicle he'd ever owned, since he'd spent a great deal of his earnings paying back student loans. There were people who mocked him for always following the rules, but that's the kind of guy he was. He just didn't see any benefit to taking short cuts when the straight and narrow got you there and did so safely.

Eyes hidden behind black, intimidating sunglasses, he stole a peek at Amy. She was staring out the window at the houses they passed, but she was wearing sunglasses as well, making it impossible to determine what she was thinking.

Probably about what an ass he'd been all day.

"Why'd Michael have to leave? Surf's up?" He sighed. Apparently he wasn't done. For the life of him, he couldn't figure out why he was determined to piss her off.

She looked over her sunglasses at him. "He had stuff to do. I didn't think you'd mind giving me a ride home. Sorry we imposed on your busy day."

The wind whipped loose strands of hair around her face but did nothing to detract from the sarcasm in her tone.

Well, that was a telling little comeback. Is that what she really thought his problem was? That he was upset because she needed a ride home?

Amy turned her head away, but snapped it back again. "What's your problem with Michael, anyway?"

Her astute observation, along with Janelle's earlier one, slammed into him, showing him that his attitude toward Michael had become obvious to others. It was bad enough to have it as a personal annoyance, but to have to explain it to everyone... Without a doubt he'd come off sounding irrational because he didn't understand it himself.

Nick braked at the four-way stop sign before making a right hand turn. "I don't have a problem with Michael." And he didn't. Not really. It's just that something about Michael wasn't quite right. Something about Michael and Amy, together, wasn't quite right. That was closer to the truth.

"Let's just forget it," he said. "I'm having a bad day, that's all." But that wasn't all, and he knew it, because his day had been terrific, until he noticed the two of them in the pool. Still, there was no sense taking it out on her. "Look, I'm sorry, okay?" He smiled at her to convince her he meant it.

"Okay," Amy said, picking at the material of her shorts. He knew he could count on her forgiving nature. "Hey, can we stop by old man Horton's pharmacy?" she asked. "I need to pick up a prescription."

"For what?" Nick asked, concern edging its way into his

gut. He gave her a quick once-over. She looked fine to him. She looked real fine, as a matter of fact. From her dark blonde hair done up in a ponytail, to her little pink polished toes peeking out from her sandals.

"Just some pills. Nothing you need to worry your pretty little head about," she said, teasing replacing her previous sarcasm.

Pills? What kind of pills? The concern in his gut tightened into a sinking feeling. If there wasn't anything wrong with her, then what could she be picking up at the pharmacy that required a prescription? In pill form.

Only one possibility presented itself. He drummed his fingers insistently on the console, but it didn't keep him from blurting out his conclusion.

"Birth control pills." He said it like the accusation it was. He couldn't help it. It wasn't until he said it out loud that he realized how much time and effort he'd spent not thinking about Michael and Amy as an… *intimate* couple.

Now all that effort was wasted as his unruly imagination took the steamy suggestion and ran with it. Who would've guessed he could have such vivid images running through his brain while he was wide awake? Visions of Amy on satin sheets, the beach…a kitchen counter. It didn't matter where. What mattered was the fact that she was naked and smiling in all of them. Smiling at Michael.

Jesus.

Amy and Michael were having sex? Blonde, no nickname, surfer dude Michael. Had things gotten that serious? Why hadn't he noticed?

Because he didn't want to.

His hands tightened on the wheel. It was none of his

business, the rational side of his brain chanted. Unfortunately, his dark, possessive side refused to listen.

For her part, Amy laughed. Actually laughed. "I am so not going to answer that." She twisted slightly toward him in her seat, the seatbelt dividing her in half diagonally between her breasts. "Look, Nick. Don't make me make you cry like I did when you were twelve and I was nine."

He pretended to let the subject drop. "You pushed me out of a tree," he reminded her.

"No, I pushed you and you fell out of a tree. Broke your arm, too, as I recall."

"And as I recall," he began, "It was I who chased you up the tree."

"No, you drove me up a tree. Just like you're doing now. Except this time, we're in a car and if I push you, we'll probably both end up wrapped around a tree." She put her hand on his arm. "So, just let it go, okay?"

Well, like it or not, Nick had his answer. He decided he didn't like it.

I told you it was none of your business, the rational side of his brain reminded him. And didn't that just top off his perfect day?

Amy watched Nick as he pulled into a parking space and unbuckled his seatbelt. His movements were always so smooth and confident. Not like hers, which were frequently so unsure.

Why was that? They'd been raised so differently from each other. With her having parents who doted on her, anyone would think she'd be the secure and confident one. Just like with his parents abandoning him to his grandmother, he should be the one unsure of his place in this world. But he wasn't. He always knew just where he was going.

Whereas Amy wasn't going anywhere. Her plans weren't really plans at all. It was her grand strategy to continue working in her family's construction company until she retired. Fortunately, she was good at finances. So good, in fact, that she'd managed to put away a nice little nest egg. Too bad she didn't know what she was going to use it for.

She frowned. Nick would know. He'd know what he was saving for before he even started saving.

Unaware of her thoughts, Nick walked around the front of the car and held the door open for her. "You don't have to come in," she said. "I'm only going to be a minute."

"I gotta pick up some…stuff," he said, swinging the door shut behind him and clicking his remote key chain twice. The car beeped that all was secure and he pocketed the keys.

She raised an eyebrow and looked back at him. "Stuff?" she couldn't help asking.

"Yeah." He took her elbow and urged her down the gum-encrusted walkway. "Man stuff."

She held the door open for him, letting it wheeze shut behind her as she entered. Sliding her sunglasses on top of her head, she said, "Just go ahead and admit you're getting nakey girly magazines, Nick. I'm a big girl, I know about these things." She walked beside him, her sandals flip-flopping as she went.

"Nakey?" he wanted to know. "I don't read 'nakey' magazines, Amy. Just how old are you?"

"Very clever." She smiled up at him. "Nobody reads nakey magazines, Nick. They're strictly for the pictures. The words are there just so you can tell yourself it's all about the articles."

The two of them made their way past the displays of camera film and candy, past magazines and make-up, all the way to the back of the store where the prescriptions were filled.

"Hi, Amy. Hi, Nick," Mr. Horton said, putting his broom against the wall and squinting at them as they stopped at the counter.

That's how it was living in a small town all your life. Everyone knew everyone else by name, and their business, too. Nick hated it, but Amy thought it was cozy. Like family.

"Oh, Nick." Mr. Horton pushed his glasses up on his nose and continued in what he probably supposed was a whisper but which she had no trouble hearing. "We have a sale on condoms if you're running low."

Amy felt like someone had punched her in the stomach. Looking over at Nick, she saw his face slowly flooding with color. Which was interesting, because she was certain her face had drained of any color.

"No, thanks, Mr. Horton," Nick managed to choke out. "I haven't finished the last batch." He thumbed randomly through a rack of cigarette lighters, even though she knew he didn't smoke.

The last batch? Nick bought condoms in batches? She stared at him, her mind racing with thoughts of Nick's busy sex life.

That his supply was still stocked didn't take away the distressing knowledge that it existed.

"Okay," Mr. Horton said. "But if you need any, you've got until the week before Christmas to get them on sale."

"Will do," Nick said at the same time Mr. Horton turned his attention on Amy.

"You here to pick up your allergy pills?"

"Yes, thank you." She put the thought of Nick's having to buy condoms on sale and in batches firmly out of her mind. It was none of her concern what he did with his private life.

She paid Mr. Horton, took the white prescription bag, and turned to go, clinging to her resolution to keep her thoughts to herself. And if she was fighting off a small tingle of excitement at the visions running through her head, that was best put to bed– *er*–forgotten as well.

Nick grabbed a roll of duct tape and paid for it quickly. Seeing her looking at him with a grin on her face, he mouthed the words, "Man stuff" as he pocketed his change.

Amy laughed and decided to buy a pack of gum at the last minute. Then a romance novel, two candy bars, and a fuzzy pen. She denied she was stalling, trying to avoid the moment she'd have to get into the car with Nick. Could she really refrain from calling him The Great Condom Baron?

The silly thought made her feel better, made the whole thing seem less threatening somehow. With her mind and her mood once more balanced, the pair made their way back to Nick's car in silence. But it was no use. Once there, she couldn't keep quiet any longer. "What was that about?" she asked casually as she buckled her seatbelt.

So much for her firm resolutions. And hadn't she just gotten done telling him to mind his own business regarding her sex life? Not that there was any comparison between the two.

He shook his head and started the car. "I have no idea." Both buckled in, he backed out of the parking space. "If I had to guess, I'd say old man Horton's trying to find a way to keep his store in business for a little while longer."

Amy thought about that and decided it was probably true. The national chains were everywhere, in all kinds of businesses. They had even started to take root in their small town. Several fast food restaurants now operated here. She could remember when the only place to get a hamburger was at a cookout, or at

The Shake Shop.

Still, against the odds, Silas Horton had managed to keep his pharmacy going and profitable for decades. A shrewd and fearless businessman, no way would he close down without a fight.

That thought made her feel marginally better only because it made her hopeful that the condom thing was Mr. Horton's idea and not Nick's proclivity. "Well, it would've been worse if he'd had tampons on sale," she said.

Nick glanced at her with a look of horror on his face. "Oh, yeah," he said. "Mr. Horton asking me if I needed to stock up on tampons would've been infinitely worse." The rakish grin that followed that comment belied his earlier look of horror.

The wind from the open sunroof ruffled his dark hair, and she took a minute to appreciate how truly good looking Nick was. She'd known him since she was a child, and he'd always been beautiful, but as a man, he was breathtaking. His hair changed hue depending on the light. Her mother called it autumn hair, with the reddish highlights buried in the almost-black strands.

His grip on the wheel was firm and steady. She could relax in Nick's presence.

His shirt flapped around him every once in awhile, drawing her attention to the definition of his chest. She knew he worked out because she and her friends had watched him when they were all at the gym together, but even if she hadn't seen him, she'd know. He had that look about him. Not bulky or strained, just smooth, hard muscle moving under warm satiny skin.

She sighed and he looked her way. A strand of hair tumbled over his forehead, mussing up his appearance enough to make him appear approachable

He turned his attention back to the road, his fingers tapping on the gearshift. "I'm sorry I gave you a hard time about the pills. It was none of my business."

"It's okay."

She wanted the drive to last a while longer, but he was pulling into her complex before she finished the last word.

It was probably one of the only times she ever got the last word with Nick.

Thanksgiving Day arrived and Amy found herself rummaging around the back of her walk-in closet, searching for her missing sandal. Sitting back on her heels, she scanned the floor. Where could it be? No matter how hard she stared, the shoe refused to appear.

Realizing the only place left to search was behind some boxes, she pulled one away from the wall. No shoe. She let out a sigh of frustration.

The next box was heavier, making her wonder what it contained. Tilting her head and squinting in the dim light she made out the packing label. *Books-paperback, keeper shelf.*

That was a reminder that under no circumstances were these books to be given, or thrown, away. They represented years of avid reading and collecting. She ought to invest in a bookcase, so she'd have somewhere respectable to store them.

Straining, she managed to push the book box over next to the first box, creating a little wall to her side. One more box to go and her shoe would either appear or remain forever lost.

The box came away from the wall easily. So easily, in fact, that Amy toppled over onto her bottom, tearing one of the cardboard flaps.

Ouch.

She tried to piece together the torn edges, but it was no use.

There were no other options but to either replace the box, actually sort through the contents and put them away, or just chuck the whole thing.

She peered into the secret depths, sneezing as dust flew into her face. She pulled out three items–a yellowed photo of her at the beach as a child, an ancient Valentine's Day card that was curled on the edges, and a smiley face pin. By the time she set those things in her lap, her fingers were grimy. She wiped them on her shorts, pleased to know what the mystery box contained.

Mementos from her childhood. She could hardly believe she'd been carrying this stuff around for almost ten years. She couldn't even remember where half of it came from.

Was she sentimental or insane? She couldn't decide. Smiling at her childhood whimsy, she reached inside for more treasures, amazed at the memories that exited the box along with the pieces of her past.

Yearbooks, hair ribbons, a trophy for winning the third grade spelling bee. Wow, this was like an archaeological dig! She hadn't seen this stuff in ages.

Digging deeper, she smiled. Framed photos of her and her friends, a crusty corsage from some prom or other, and various pieces of costume jewelry. In just a short time every available space around her was covered in items she'd sorted into designated "keep" and "toss" groups until finally, only one thing remained.

Her high school diary. She pulled the book out, not recognizing it at first. Not until she saw the gilt lock on the side, the clasp forever torn away and missing. She couldn't remember how the lock had been destroyed, but she definitely remembered the little book.

The only diary she'd ever faithfully kept.

She ran her fingers over the padded cover before opening it slowly. The pages lifted up in a clump, age and neglect sticking them together in stubborn defiance. Peeling the obstinate edges apart carefully she managed to separate them, although they were still stiff and unyielding, as if determined to keep their juvenile secrets.

Tucking a strand of hair behind her ear, she smiled. As if she had any secrets to keep.

No sooner did the thought form than her eyes focused on the top of the very first page. Written in big black letters she read, "Amy Gilbert loves Nick Granger." She sucked in her breath, unable to believe her eyes. But there it was, screaming out at her from the past.

Most people got over their childhood crushes, but she loved Nick even into adulthood. She'd tried to get beyond it. Many times, even. But no matter who she went out with and tried to love, she spent all her time comparing him to Nick.

All those years of stifled emotions, and here she was, still stuck in this unrequited rut.

For a long time she thought she'd finally accepted this as her lot in life. She even rationalized that if she couldn't have her one true love, she could be happy settling for a close second.

However sad that reality was, she believed she'd found this person in the body of her current boyfriend, Michael. He was everything Nick wasn't.

Running a cautious finger over the page, she traced the individual letters of her childhood confession, her eyes filling with tears she was too grown-up now to shed. How had she come so far, only to still be in the same place?

Nick was going to make some woman a wonderful husband

some day. Now she supposed it would be some woman she didn't know, since he was taking a job that moved him to another state. She would miss having him all to herself.

Can't miss what you've never had.

Amy's heart picked up speed and she took in a quick breath as a forbidden thought took control of her good sense. Could she do it? Could she have her way with him before he left? It was a possibility she'd always toyed with, in the back of her mind, but never had the nerve or opportunity to pursue.

What do you have to lose? one side of her brain argued.

Only her peace of mind, the other side answered.

She scoffed. Like she had any peace of mind—at least not where Nick was concerned.

What about Michael? her conscience spoke up.

Oh, yeah. She'd forgotten about him for a minute. Guilt over her remiss quelled the lascivious meanderings. Thank goodness for a conscience that wouldn't let her get herself into trouble.

Amy, so good and true that she's still a virgin at twenty-seven.

What's wrong with that? her sensible side wanted to know.

Amy cringed inwardly. It was true! She was the only twenty-seven year old virgin she knew. Her life was such a cartoon at times.

It wasn't that she hadn't had plenty of offers, and had even accepted a few of them over the years, starting in high school. But somehow, when it came right down to actually doing it, she couldn't come through.

The first change of mind had ended badly, with the guy calling her names and ranting on about her being a tease. The humiliation was so fierce it was almost a year before she considered taking the plunge again.

Once again, she chickened out. Well, not totally. A night-duty cop had actually interrupted them. One who knew her parents. He swore he wouldn't tell them, but Amy lived in fear for weeks afterward.

Maybe those incidents impacted her negatively because after that, saying "no" became a little easier each time, and before she knew it, a pattern was established.

I'm saving myself for marriage, she argued back, defending her pristine condition at such an advanced age.

Oh, you are not. You're saving yourself for Nick, and you always have been. Why won't you admit it?

She stiffened in the sudden, overwhelming shock of realization

No! There was no way.

But she knew it was true. She'd been waiting around for Nick forever. Saving herself for the time when he would notice she was grown up and all his. Never making a plan, never having a real life, always waiting and hoping. And not even being courageous enough to admit it.

There you go. Now, what are you going to do about it, girly? the daring side of her asked. A daring side she hadn't even known she possessed, and now it threatened to take control.

Do? She didn't know what to do. What could she do? She had a boyfriend already. Would it be fair to sleep with the man she truly wanted, while the one she should be giving herself to waited in the wings?

If she was suddenly ready to go through with it, why not Michael? He was the logical choice. But the problem was, she wasn't feeling logical right now. She was feeling gypped, shortchanged, cheated. Damn it, it was *her* virginity, why couldn't she give it to whoever she wanted to? She and Michael weren't married, weren't even engaged, and while she enjoyed his company and was willing to see where the relationship went, he didn't own her.

You're rationalizing, the sensible side chimed in.

I know, she agreed. And it's working. Anticipation squashed the guilt.

"Amy? You in there?" a voice called from the doorway of her bedroom.

Jerking upright she threw the diary back into the box, scraping the back of her hand across her eyes and wiping at tears she couldn't shed.

Now was not the time for a confrontation with Michael. They had to be at Ted's house for holiday dinner, and she wouldn't ruin the day for everyone else.

"Michael!" she said, surprise evident in her voice. "Just looking for my lost shoe." Checking the empty space behind the memento box, she was relieved to see her sandal. Grabbing it, she held it up before putting it on.

"What's all this?" Michael asked, nodding his head at the various items piled around the closet.

Amy snatched them up and madly tossed them back into the box. "Just stuff from high school. Junk I need to get rid of, but I don't have time to mess with right now." She hated being caught off-guard.

Folding down the three flaps she pushed it back against the wall, followed by the other two boxes. He watched, an amused smile on his face.

Standing up, she brushed her hands together. "There." She walked past him into the bedroom, taking his attention with her.

He gently took hold of her chin and wiped at her forehead.

"You've got a black streak just above your eyes."

She held her breath while he looked at her closely, knowing the streak came from brushing at her eyes, and praying he wouldn't see the trace of tears. "Are you ready to go?" she asked, clearly a diversionary tactic, but one he wouldn't realize she was using.

"That's why I'm here." He let go of her and stepped back. "It's a good thing you gave me a key. I knocked several times, but I guess you didn't hear me."

Amy refrained from reminding him that he had hounded her for a key. At first, she'd resisted, not comfortable with him being able to invade her private space whenever he wanted. But as time went on, and Michael kept insisting, she finally gave in. She wasn't happy about it, then or now, but she was used to it. And it wasn't like he took advantage of the situation. No, Michael was very respectful of her privacy, as she was of his. They got along well that way.

"No, I guess I didn't." Amy turned off the light in the closet before shutting the doors, determined to protect her secret. The decision to do something about her feelings for Nick was too new, her confidence far too fragile to risk discovery. And Michael was a very real part of her life that she'd have to deal with if she was going to carry this out. But not now.

"Well, if you're ready, I guess we might as well go."

He tilted his head and looked at her. "Why are you so nervous?"

"I'm not." She twisted a strand of blonde hair around her finger, fidgeting under his perusal. "I just want to get going. We're already late."

"We're always late," he reminded her. "Speaking of dinner, I hate to do this, but I'm going to have to leave early. I've got tons of paperwork due tomorrow, and if I don't get busy on it today, there's no way it'll be finished. Do you think Nick can give you a ride home?"

Before she could stop them, her eyebrows flew up. "Again?" she said. "This is becoming a habit, isn't it?" Not that she was truly objecting, she was simply making an observation.

"Yeah, I know. But business is business." He avoided her eyes and the platitude rolled off his tongue as he looked her over. "You look great!"

He nodded his head slowly, his gaze running over her as he wiggled his eyebrows at her lasciviously. "You look better than great, as a matter of fact."

Amy could feel herself coloring up at the comment, a feeling of pleasure suffusing her. "You don't look so bad yourself," she said, knowing how Michael enjoyed compliments. And the truth was he did look good.

He pulled her into his arms. "That's why we're such a terrific couple. We complement each other so well."

Amy thought about it for a second and agreed. They did complement each other. And Michael wanted her, the way a man in a relationship wants a woman. Maybe she should reconsider this Nick thing?

He lowered his head to hers and she realized she hadn't kissed him when he appeared. His lips met hers and she waited for something to happen.

And something did.

The realization that someone as wonderful as Michael was interested in her warmed her all the way to her toes, although the area of her heart remained lukewarm.

He soon lifted his head and turned away, causing Amy to acknowledge to herself that the entire kiss had passed with no participation from her. She placed her fingertips on her lips, but didn't say anything.

Not that she needed to. It wasn't until they were on their way she realized Michael hadn't even noticed.

Chapter Three

Thanksgiving dinner at Janelle's consisted of all the traditional dishes, plus a few created by Janelle herself.

The guests seated around the table waited for the blessing to be said before digging in. Nick sneaked a peak at the expectant faces and smiled. The children were seated at their own little table just off from the main one. A designation guaranteed to make them feel all grown up and independent of their mother's insisting they eat their vegetables and drink their milk.

With the very last "amen" still echoing around the room, sweet potatoes and turkey were passed around. Ted and Janelle occupied the ends of the table, while Nick sat on Janelle's left next to an elderly neighbor, Mrs. Sigmund, who'd been invited because Janelle said no one should be alone on Thanksgiving. Across from Nick and Mrs. Sigmund sat Amy and Michael, engrossed in putting food on each other's plates.

In fact, if Nick wanted to, he could kick Michael under the table and everyone would consider it an accident. And he might, if they didn't quit making such a spectacle of themselves.

"Aren't they sweet?" elderly Mrs. Sigmund sighed into Nick's ear.

"Yes, disgustingly so," Nick mumbled.

"What's that, dear? I couldn't quite hear you." She leaned into him, her hand cupped around her ear.

"I agreed with you, Mrs. Sigmund," he picked up a bowl,

"and I asked if you'd like some stuffing."

"Oh, my heavens yes." She held her plate out to him. He spooned some stuffing onto her plate, along with a few slices of turkey, some cranberry sauce, and a mixed vegetable dish that didn't look too appetizing to Nick. Before he knew it, she was spooning food onto his plate and the two of them were a caricature of the Michael and Amy show.

"*Aw*, aren't they sweet?" he heard Michael say in Amy's ear, making no attempt to keep his voice down.

Amy giggled. "Mrs. Sigmund, you'd better watch out. I hear Nick's quite the ladies' man. I heard it from Mr. Horton at the pharmacy." She tucked a strand of hair behind her ear and winked at Nick.

"My dear," Mrs. Sigmund said, "Maybe it's Nick who should watch out for me." She tucked the strap from her glasses behind her ear and winked back at Amy.

The table burst into laughter at Nick's expense, with Michael laughing the loudest.

Nick gripped his fork and stuffed mashed potatoes into his mouth to keep from telling Michael where he could stuff his. No matter how he tried, he just couldn't like the guy.

"So, Nick," Ted said. "Why don't you like that guy?"

Nick's head spun around so fast the passing air roared in his ears. "What did you say?" he croaked. Surely he hadn't heard Ted correctly.

"I asked you if you'd like some pie. You know, after you're finished with your meal. Which should be any second now, the way you're shoveling it in."

Nick flushed, relieved to find Ted wasn't a mind reader after all. "Oh, it's just that it's all so good, isn't it Mrs. Sigmund?" He turned to his dinner partner for help.

"Yes, it is," she gamely jumped to his rescue. "And Janelle, if you could give me the recipe for your stuffing, I'd appreciate it. I don't believe I've ever tasted anything like it."

Janelle beamed. "You know I will. But really, there's nothing to it. I just make it the traditional way, then add a couple of diced apples." She sipped at her drink. "I find stuffing to be such a versatile dish. So many ways to prepare it."

She launched into an impressive speech on the virtues of stuffing, how it could be utilized for any holiday, giving Nick a chance to surreptitiously watch the couple across from him.

They seemed oblivious to everyone around them. At least, Michael did. Amy looked like she wanted to enjoy her meal in peace, without him fawning over her. Nick half suspected that Michael's attention was for show.

Deciding with difficulty that they were none of his concern, Nick focused on his meal, and everyone ate quietly, the chattering of the children the only sound.

"I know," Mrs. Sigmund exclaimed during the lull in conversation. "Why don't we go around the table telling everyone what we're thankful for?"

Nick almost groaned out-loud, but it was the sound of Michael's fork clanging against his plate that caught everyone's attention.

"That sounds terrific," he said, using his napkin to wipe gravy off his chin, then scooting his chair back. "But I'm afraid I'm going to have to take a rain check on that one."

Nick looked at Michael's plate to find it empty. And Ted thought *he* had been shoveling it in?

The other man pushed his chair in, turning to his hostess. "It was wonderful, Janelle. My stomach thanks you." He patted his middle for emphasis. "But I've got to go. I hate to eat and run, but there's just no way around it, I'm afraid."

Nick's attention spiked joyfully while the others murmured objections. The day was looking up after all!

"But, but..." Mrs. Sigmund *tsked*, while Nick found himself grinding his teeth and hoping his dining companion wasn't about to spoil this godsend. "If you leave, it'll ruin the whole atmosphere of the party."

Nick nodded in agreement. A change of atmosphere was exactly what he was counting on.

"Nonsense, Mrs. Sigmund." Janelle jumped up as she spoke. "I know this seems abrupt, but the truth is, Michael took time off from his hectic schedule to be here. Ted and I knew he wouldn't be able to linger."

She patted the older woman's shoulder as she walked past. "I'm so sorry you have to leave, Michael, but at least let me get you some pie." She started toward the kitchen, her voice trailing off as she listed the varieties she had on hand.

Michael followed her and silence shrouded the dining room until one of the boys spilled his milk. Chaos ensued as Ted tried to mop up the mess and Mrs. Sigmund toddled over to give him her napkin and her advice. Nick smiled at Amy and tried to think of something to say, but Janelle was back before he could think of anything.

Thirty seconds later the milk mess was cleaned up, everyone regained their seats, and Michael stood at the back of Amy's chair massaging her neck. "Well, everyone, it's been real, but I've got to leave. Ames," he said, giving her hair a little tug. "Come see me off?"

"Sure." She rose and pushed her chair in.

Nick watched her walk out of the dining room. From where he sat he had a clear view of the front door, and although he knew he shouldn't spy on them, he couldn't help it.

The couple paused in the foyer instead of saying their goodbyes outside. With wrapped pie in one hand, Michael used his other to tilt Amy's chin. Leaning down to kiss her, he pulled her in close while her she put her hands on his shoulders. Nick told himself it looked at first like she was pushing him away, but that didn't make sense.

They stayed together that way for long enough to make Nick's blood pressure shoot up, but not long enough to make him look away.

Finally, Michael slid his free arm down her back to cup her bottom, lifting her onto her toes and pulling her in tight to him. Nick's jaw clenched and his eyes burned. It was all he could do to keep himself seated.

"Jealous?" Janelle asked from his side.

"What?" he asked, tearing himself away from the scene going on in the foyer.

"I asked if you wanted some relish." She passed him her special recipe chutney.

"Thanks." He spooned some onto his mixed vegetables. "Why do you call it relish?" he asked when he was done, while still keeping tabs on the couple in the foyer.

"Because that's what you do when you eat it. You relish it." She grinned at him. "Now that Amy's back, let's go with Mrs. Sigmund's suggestion and tell everyone what we're thankful for. I'll go first."

Nick determined to be the last one to offer up his thanks because it would take him that long to come up with something besides, "I'm thankful Michael left."

* * *

Janelle leaned toward the mirror and applied lipstick for the third time. The light in the powder room wasn't the most flattering, but this was as close to the foyer as she could get without actually hovering at the front door.

Tilting her head to one side she checked her overall appearance, pleased she'd decided to wear her dangling silver earrings instead of something gold and conservative. She wanted tonight to be special. Not that it could be otherwise, of course, but she wanted Ted to remember both the night and her as beautiful and exciting, not dull and settled.

But making a lasting impression on Ted wasn't her only mission tonight. She was also entering into the world of meddling in other people's affairs and wasn't sure how Ted would feel about that. Was she truly helping two people she loved, or was she making a big deal out of something that only existed in her imagination?

She frowned, then absently rubbed away the wrinkles between her brows with manicured fingertips. She wasn't concerned about the creases the lines made. What did she care about a few marks here and there? She wasn't some shallow girl straight out of high school.

No, Janelle frowned because she'd planned this evening to serve two purposes, and so far, things weren't proceeding as smoothly as she'd hoped. She should've known Amy wouldn't be on time. She never was. The fact that she was only ten minutes late didn't matter, because even that was putting a serious crimp in Janelle's machinations.

How anyone in Ted's family ever managed to fall in love and get married, not to mention stay married, was beyond her. They were all so casual about it. As if love rained down willy-nilly on people instead of being something a person should seek and treasure. Love required some effort to grow, some tenderness to flourish, and attention in order for it to bloom.

She knew these things at an early age and made sure she pursued the possibilities. Sometimes those possibilities paid off, like with Ted, and sometimes they didn't. The chance of winning always outweighed the fear of losing.

Amy was just like Ted, and Janelle supposed it wasn't her fault, coming from laid-back parents. She loved them all dearly, but some days, she just wanted to shake them.

However, Nick had no excuse. That man possessed more perseverance than anyone else she knew. His problem was he spent all his energy pursuing dreams that led him away from real, lasting happiness. He was in constant pursuit of the very thing that was right under his nose.

Clearly if anyone was going to see the obvious around here, she would have to take great care to point it out. But in a subtle way, of course. After all, no one likes to be told what to do. Even her fourth graders balked at being ordered around arbitrarily. Janelle had learned to be diplomatic in achieving her goals, large or small. Determined, but diplomatic.

Her real problem was Ted. Yes, dear, sweet, wonderful, clueless Ted. How was he going to feel about her sticking her nose into his best friend's life? Not to mention his sister's?

An abrupt knock on the door interrupted her one-sided conversation. "Janelle, are you coming out of there?" Ted asked at the same time the doorbell rang and her chance to call the whole thing off passed.

She stuffed her lipstick into her purse, patted her hair, and opened the door, just in time to see Ted's puzzled face as he ushered Amy into the house.

"Amy?" he asked. "What are you doing here?" The confusion on his face caused Janelle to bite her bottom lip, until she remembered the three coats of lipstick she'd applied. She scrubbed a finger across her front teeth to make sure they were clean of color, then pulled her purse strap onto her shoulder and waited for the ax to fall.

"I'm babysitting, of course," she responded, and then unwittingly changed the direction of the conversation. "Janelle, you look gorgeous! I love it when you wear your hair loose down your back like that."

"Thanks." Janelle shot Ted a glance, hoping he would be distracted by Amy's comment.

"But, I thought–" he was cut off by the boys' boisterous entry into the fray.

"Aunt Amy, Aunt Amy," they chimed in their little singsong voices, each one trying to get to her first. Amy picked Jacob up, shifting him awkwardly onto one hip, and put her other arm around Kevin's shoulders, continuous practice since they were babies helping her balance their demands. Jacob was getting too big to be hoisted onto a hip, his chubby legs dangling down to Amy's knee proved that, but Amy didn't seem to notice, and Jacob wasn't complaining either.

"Well, boys! Is it okay if you babysit me tonight while your mom and dad go out to dinner?" She ruffled Kevin's hair with her free hand, eliciting a grin from the boy.

Amy's easy way with the children brought a lump to Janelle's throat and strengthened her conviction. This standoff between Amy and Nick had gone on long enough. Somebody had to do something, and if that somebody must be her, then so be it.

"Kevin, Jacob, you boys know Aunt Amy is the boss, right?" Janelle put her hands on her hips and raised one eyebrow.

"Your mother's right. You both are to do what Aunt Amy says," Ted added his agreement to Janelle's decree, but Janelle knew he wasn't done quizzing her about why Amy was here.

Both boys nodded, and Amy winked at Kevin. "Janelle, if you guys have to tell them I'm the boss, then we've got a problem," she said with a laugh as Jacob thrust his unwrapped lollipop into her face.

Setting him on the floor, she flexed her arm a few times and Janelle knew from experience she was relieving muscles tired from holding the boy.

Once she unwrapped the lollipop for Jacob, Amy handed it back to him. He wasted no time popping the candy into his mouth, his "thank you" coming out garbled. "Looks like I got here just in the nick of time." Amy rested her hand on Jacob's head, as if to assure him she was still available if he wanted her.

"Speaking of the Nick of time," Ted interrupted, but Janelle grabbed his arm and tugged him to the door.

"With Amy here, we can go now, Ted. Hurry up, or we'll be late. I don't want to waste our reservations." She babbled as she opened the door and bent to kiss the boys goodbye. She barely let Ted do the same before she pushed him through the doorway. "Amy, I left instructions on where we can be reached, and you know Ted's cell phone number. The boys have had their baths, they just want to watch TV for a little while, then you can put them to bed. We shouldn't be home before midnight, so don't expect us until at least then." Out of breath from her hasty speech, she ended by pantomiming a kiss; all the while hoping her assurance that Amy and Nick would have the house to themselves wouldn't be obvious once the evening wore on.

Before she could shut the door, Ted fired a question. "What's going on, Janelle? I thought Nick was babysitting?"

Janelle shushed Ted and then peeked back into the foyer through the small crack where the door was still open. Amy had already taken the boys toward the back of the house. Closing the door tightly, she turned sheepishly to Ted. Here it comes. He might be an easygoing guy, but that didn't mean he was a pushover. "Nick is babysitting," she admitted. Here came the tricky part–getting Ted to go along with it. "But so is Amy."

The pair walked down the path to the driveway. "I don't understand. Why did you have me call Nick and ask him to babysit if Amy was going to? We don't need two sitters, do we?" He shoved his hands into his pockets and kept walking, but his attention remained on her.

Before she could answer, Nick headed up the path toward them. "Nick," Janelle said breathlessly. Honestly, all this excitement couldn't be good for someone in her delicate condition. So she'd set the two of them up. It wasn't like she was doing something truly terrible. She just wanted them to give each other a chance. Was that so wrong?

Nick paused in front of them, his hesitating steps indicating his confusion. "Why are you guys out here? Who's with the boys?" His arm gestured to the house.

"Oh, Amy popped by," Janelle said, thinking fast. "We figured we'd go ahead and get going so we don't have to rush." She all but groaned aloud. So much for thinking fast. Maybe she should've thought this part of the plan out a little more carefully. Her excuses were sounding downright lame.

Ted opened his mouth and Janelle gave Nick a little push. "Go ahead up to the house, Nick, we've got to get going. Amy knows where all the instructions are, she'll show you. Bye." She knew she was acting strange, but she didn't know what else to do. She had to get Ted and Nick separated before Ted did something disturbing. Like apologizing to Nick for having him agree to babysit tonight for nothing.

Ted waited until Nick was out of earshot before he turned to her. "I'm not going anywhere until you tell me what the heck is going on. Why are we suddenly playing fast and loose with other people's time?"

Uh-oh. He'd blocked her path and crossed his arms. Ted's way of presenting an immovable object to her irresistible force.

She sighed, knowing what was coming. "I'm trying to arrange for them to be alone together. Without us around to run interference."

"Why do they need to be alone together?" From the tone of his voice, she could tell he was getting that stubborn streak fired up. His whole family might be easy to get along with, most of the time, but when they wanted to, they could be more obstinate than any mule ever born.

Janelle peeked at him. Sure enough, he stood there, waiting. Fine, she'd spill the whole story, but he was going to have to wait until they were at least seated at the restaurant and appetizers had been ordered. She was starving. All this sneaking around was strenuous.

Besides, the whole night wasn't about Nick and Amy. She and Ted had their own reason to want to be alone. And celebrate. Ted just didn't know it yet.

Wrapping her arms around his waist, she relaxed as his arms went around her in response. When he kissed the top of her head she silently thanked God she'd had the good sense to go after Ted Gilbert with everything she possessed. She was even more grateful that he'd stood still to let her catch him.

"Ted, I'm hungry. Can we finish this discussion over a shrimp cocktail and candlelight?" she asked. "I promise if you feed me, I'll be yours to command."

Ted laughed. "Okay, I know when I'm being diverted, but that doesn't mean I'll forget."

When they were both in the car, Ted made his own demands. "As soon as the appetizers arrive, it's time to tell me what's going on."

"Deal," Janelle agreed, glad when they were finally on their way because she wasn't kidding. She really was starving.

* * *

Amy took the boys into the family room and settled them onto the couch before going to the bookcase that doubled as a video stand. She knew which one was their favorite because they watched it every time she babysat.

Pulling the video from its case she put it into the VCR and busied herself adjusting the tracking. By the time the opening credits rolled, Amy was seated on the couch with one little boy snuggling on each side, wondering what Nick was doing tonight. She knew Michael was unavailable, claiming some sketchy business problem he had to take care of. She was so used to that occurrence she didn't even think about it anymore.

However, the idea of Nick's prolific use of condoms hadn't left her mind since that day in the pharmacy. For thirteen days her imagination tormented her with the knowledge.

Now, she figured the whole thing was a way for Mr. Horton to unload his merchandise, but that didn't change the fact that she couldn't forget Nick even had condoms. And if he had them, it was reasonable to assume he must use them.

She couldn't get over that part.

Man, she really was pathetic. Did she truly believe Nick was celibate? Come on, he was practically the hottest guy in town. All of Amy's friends had at one time or another either wanted to date him, or had dated him.

No, she didn't believe he was celibate. But she wanted to. Now she couldn't, because his red face in the pharmacy that day proved just how naïve her thoughts on the subject were.

"Uncle Nick," Jacob yelled, spinning around. Amy almost cracked her neck turning to see if Nick had somehow materialized in the room.

Judging by her increased breathing and her tingling awareness, it was true. Drat all the thinking she'd been doing about him, now she couldn't even think straight. "Nick, what are you doing here?" Well, that came out only slightly breathy.

He leaned his big body against the doorframe, all nonchalant male, looking good enough to make Amy sigh in response. She bit it back and stood instead, brushing her hands against her shorts in order to keep them from fidgeting around as she struggled to gain her composure. Composure that shouldn't even be lost.

This was ridiculous! For heaven's sake, she'd known this man all her life. Why was she acting so juvenile?

But the feelings skittering up her spine sure didn't feel juvenile and if she didn't get hold of herself in about two seconds flat, the repressed excitement and needs of a lifetime were going to be embarrassing. "Did you stop by on your way to a hot date?" she asked when he didn't respond to her first question.

Too late. As if excitement and need hadn't been quite enough to deal with, her emotions had degenerated into possessiveness, culminating in a jealous outburst that was way too revealing to her ears.

She forced a grin onto her face to lessen the damage, but Nick, damn him, didn't even notice her standing there. Which worked in her favor because if he spared her one lingering look, she would probably have jumped his bones.

This time she went ahead and sighed, knowing full well she would do no such thing. The entire situation was hopeless. Unfortunately, she seemed to be the only one who hadn't fully accepted it.

"No hot date tonight, I'm afraid. I'm going to be hanging out with my best buds in the whole world, watching wrestling and guzzling apple juice."

"*Yippee*." Kevin jumped up and down on the couch. "Can me and Jacob come too, Uncle Nick? Can we? We love wrestling and apple juice. We'll be good. Honest."

Nick laughed and crossed the room to lift Kevin into the air. The seven-year-old grabbed tightly to Nick's forearms, squealing first in delight and then in mock fear as Nick spun him around over his head.

"Do me, Uncle Nick, do me next," Jacob demanded, running around the room in excitement, his arms spread wide, airplane-style.

Nick put Kevin down and gave Jacob his turn, although Jacob wasn't as freewheeling about the whole thing, clinging to Nick with both his arms and his legs. He didn't seem to mind that he was missing out on being lifted over Nick's head. Judging by his childish giggles, he just wanted the experience of spinning.

Once both boys were equally dizzy and settled back on the couch, Nick turned to Amy, only slightly out of breath. Shaking his head side to side, he said to the children, "You could come with me, but I'm not going anywhere. I'm going to stay here with you guys until your mom and dad get home." He waited for their response.

Amy stared, not sure how this mix-up had happened, while

Kevin gave a brief yell. Jacob popped his lollipop out of his mouth. "Does that mean Aunt Amy has to go home?" he asked solemnly, his tongue blue from the candy.

Nick looked at her. "That depends on your Aunt Amy," he said. "Well, Amy? Do you want to hang out with us guys, watching wrestling and guzzling apple juice? I gotta warn you, there might be spontaneous spectator wrestling going on."

"Yeah, come on, Aunt Amy," Kevin pleaded. "It'll be fun. I promise to let you win if we wrestle." His little face wrinkled earnestly in his attempt to woo her.

"Nick, there seems to be some sort of mistake. Janelle called me to see if I could babysit tonight. Why would she do that if you were going to?" It didn't make sense. Janelle wasn't a flighty sort; she'd never make a mistake like this.

Nick shrugged, his shoulders causing the bottom of his nubby shirt to rise up slightly as he did. "I don't know about Janelle. Ted's the one who called me and asked."

Well, that made sense. Her brother would make a mistake like that. She shook her head to clear away the meaningless pondering. What did it matter anyway?

She looked at the three of them staring at her and knew she didn't have a better offer. In fact, she couldn't even think of anything better than to spend an entire evening alone with Nick and her nephews. The idea of wrestling later intrigued her, but she knew Nick didn't mean anything sexual by it. Which was certainly a shame.

"Okay, I'll stay, since I told your parents I'd babysit tonight, but if we're having apple juice, then I insist we have popcorn too. It's only fair." She didn't have to wait long for their response.

The boys jumped up and down in agreement and Nick raised his left hand to his brow. "You are a brave woman. I salute you," he said, pretending all seriousness.

"You're raising the wrong hand, Uncle Nick," Kevin whispered, tugging on Nick's shirt, the movement tightening the material over his chest. The shirt wasn't made of sturdy material and the impossible thought crossed Amy's mind that with a little more effort it could probably be ripped right off his body.

Whew, Amy, you have to get control of your imagination.

"Yeah, you gotta use your other hand," Jacob agreed, raising his hand to show Nick how it was done.

"Oh, sorry," Nick said, and promptly switched.

The deal sealed, they stopped the movie, and with fifteen minutes to spare before wrestling began, they headed to the kitchen to make popcorn and get their juice.

Amy surreptitiously watched Nick with the boys. Hefting Jacob into his arms, he leaned a hip against the counter. She listened closely to what they were saying while Kevin was busy focusing on getting the juice out of the refrigerator.

"Hey, Uncle Nick," Jacob said, grabbing Nick's face with his little hands to garner his attention. "Guess what I can do."

"What can you do?" he asked, a grin on his face and encouragement in his eyes. Her heart skipped a beat in response to the obvious love she saw on Nick's face.

"I can do this." Jacob proceeded to wiggle his eyebrows up and down rapidly. "Can you do that?"

Nick threw his head back and laughed before showing Jacob that he could indeed. She smiled. Nick's forehead creased and uncreased with his movements. Jacob laughed and hugged his neck in childish approval.

She thought she couldn't be more impressed with Nick's tender care. She was wrong.

He put Jacob on the floor before casually asking him, "How

long do you suppose that lollipop's going to last?"

Amy had to agree with Nick's assessment of the situation. Jacob was the only kid she knew who would suck a lollipop into nothingness instead of chomping it to pieces after a while. The result was that as the candy got smaller, the stick shredded, and his face got downright gooey. It would be better to clean him up before the match began instead of during.

"I don't know." Jacob removed the lollipop and studied it, little flecks of white paper stuck to his chin. "It's probably going to make my popcorn taste funny, huh?"

"I don't know. It might." Nick leaned on the counter and treated the four-year-old to all of his attention. Kevin was helping Amy set the cups up to receive their fill of juice. From the corner of her eye she watched Jacob ponder the problem.

"Uncle Nick," Jacob began, holding out the lollipop to Nick. "Would you help me finish it?" His eyes were focused on Nick's and Amy held her breath.

"*Ew*, that's gross, Jacob," Kevin said in complete candor.

Jacob dropped his arm quickly to his side. "Never mind," he said, sheepishly, lowering his gaze to his toes.

Nick bent down before him and raised his chin, taking the lollipop out of Jacob's hand. With only a slight hesitation he popped it into his own mouth. "Of course I will," he said around the candy. "Isn't that what best buds do?" He stood and ruffled Jacob's hair with his big hand while she struggled to keep from bursting into grateful tears right there.

He looked so ridiculous with that little white, shredded stick hanging from the corner of his mouth, she wanted to laugh. Except she couldn't. Emotion clogged her throat and she pressed her fingertips to her lips to still their slight quiver. It was all she could do to keep those tears unshed.

"Kevin," she finally said, her voice husky and unrecognizable. "Why don't you and Jacob take our drinks into the family room? Uncle Nick and I will be right there, soon as the popcorn's done." Fortunately, the lollipop incident didn't seem to make as big an impact on the boys as it had on her, and they anxiously agreed to the task.

With the boys holding a cup in each hand, they left the room. Amy looked at Nick. She wanted to say something, but wasn't sure what. "You are a good man, Nick Granger, to spare a little boy's feelings." It wasn't clever or meaningful, but it was true, and that would have to do.

He took the lollipop out of his mouth, and looking over his shoulder, wrapped the candy in a paper towel and threw it surreptitiously into the trashcan. "Anybody would've done the same thing," he replied over his shoulder as he left.

He could be modest if he wanted, but Amy could name exactly two men who would have done what Nick did, and one of those men was Jacob's father.

His gentle treatment of Jacob's feelings almost made her wish she was brave enough to trust him with hers.

Chapter Four

Amy sat safely on the couch, her knees to her chest, watching the wrestling match taking place on the floor in front of her. The coffee table was pushed back against the wall and the chairs were shoved to the side in an attempt to keep from hurting the contestants, but also so damage to the furniture was minimal.

From where she sat, nibbling the last of the popcorn, it looked like the boys were getting the best of Nick. They had him on the carpet, sprawled on his back, with Jacob holding his legs down and Kevin sitting on his chest, his little hands pressing Nick's shoulders flat, making sure his back was on the ground.

Forgetting the popcorn in her hand, she let her gaze roam appreciatively over Nick's body, his horizontal position affording her an outstanding vantage point, and she used it to scope out his masculine attributes.

Such as broad shoulders made for bearing the burdens of every day life, or the weight of two small boys demanding a ride. The thought made her smile, although she managed to hold back a sigh.

She continued down over his chest, marveling at just how impressive Nick had become as a man. As a boy, there was promise of things to come, but that promise fully realized was a sight to behold, and she was beholding all she could.

One of the boys had caused Nick's shirt to ride up, so Amy had an unimpeded view of his stomach, and the sight of its tanned expanse caught her eye. She let her gaze follow the trail of hair that descended from his navel to the button of his jeans, sucking in a breath as she moved over the zipper. Quickly, before she gave herself away, she moved on to the length of his legs, wishing he was wearing shorts.

"Count, Aunt Amy, hurry up," Kevin yelled in a panic as Nick moved.

She jerked herself forward on the cushion where she was sitting. "Oh, sorry." She'd forgotten she was supposed to be refereeing this match. "One," she began, and Nick gave a low growl. "Two," she continued, as Nick lifted his shoulders off the ground slightly, only to fall back again. The boys squealed and Jacob yelled, "Count faster, Aunt Amy, he's getting loose."

"Three!" she pronounced, just as Nick rolled both boys over onto the floor, the three of them laughing all the way.

"We won," Kevin announced. "Your back was down when she got to three, Uncle Nick. We beat you fair and square."

"I don't think so," Nick argued. "I'm pretty sure I had a shoulder up."

"*Nuh-uh*," Jacob joined the fray. "I saw the whole thing, Uncle Nick. You were down for the whole count. You were!" He frowned and jammed his fists onto his hips to emphasize his point.

Amy watched her nephews argue their case like seasoned attorneys, but Nick remained unmoved. He sat up and stretched his arms over his head, working the kinks out of his back. "I'm afraid I'm going to have to demand a rematch. I think I was robbed," he claimed, but the boys were having none of it. They'd wrestled enough to know when someone was trying to steal their victory. In fact, it was part of the game.

"Aunt Amy, you saw the whole thing, too. We won, didn't

we?" Both boys raced over to where she sat, convinced she would back up their claim, but the truth was, she had no idea if Nick's shoulders were on the floor. At the time, she'd been too busy watching his front to notice his back.

Still, she was the referee; her call was the final say-so. "You sure did," she gave the boys their victory and she gave it to them in good measure. "In fact, his whole body was pinned to the mat. He couldn't move a single muscle." Kevin's quick, appreciative hug outweighed the exaggerated noises of protest Nick was making.

"There, see?" They turned on Nick. "Told you we won." Together they waited for Nick to concede.

But Nick wasn't budging. He sat back on the floor and crossed his arms over his chest. "Nope," he said. "I was robbed, and I'm not getting up off this floor until I get my rematch. Winner gets cookies and no way I'm losing out on that."

He looked so ridiculous sitting there, Amy wondered how anyone could take him seriously, but apparently the boys did.

They looked at her, their brows furrowed, concerned that if they wrestled again they might lose the promised prize. "You wrestle him, Aunt Amy," Jacob said out of the blue. It took Kevin about two seconds to agree with the idea, and unexpectedly she was the focus of three pairs of eyes.

Amy looked to Nick, ready to call the whole thing a draw.

He raised a brow at her in invitation. "Yeah, you wrestle me, Aunt Amy. Winner gets cookies *and* ice cream."

"What does the loser get?" Amy asked, but her heart wasn't into the question. The image of her rolling around on the floor with Nick was doing strange things to her pulse and her breathing, and even the part of her mind that was trying to remain rational couldn't help chanting that this was a win-win situation.

"I don't know." Nick looked to the boys. "What does the loser get?"

"Loser gets oatmeal!" Kevin proclaimed it as a fate worse than death.

"With raisins," Jacob added torture to the mix.

"Well, there you have it," Nick said. "Winner gets cookies and ice cream, loser gets oatmeal and raisins. Is it a deal?" He put out his hand to shake on it.

She sucked in a lungful of air before reminding herself this wasn't any kind of come-on from Nick's point of view, and he wasn't going to put the moves on her while he had her pinned. It was just a little wrestling match for the boys' sake. As long as she remembered that, everything would be fine.

Nick got onto his knees. "Come on, Amy. I'll go easy on you."

Oh, that did it. Lust was something she could overlook. A challenge to her skill at physical contact sports was something else. She'd show him who knew how to wrestle. She could cheat better than anyone.

Once on the floor and into position she pulled the front of her T-shirt out and twisted it. Catching Nick's interested gaze, she smirked and raised it above her ribs. From the corner of her eye she could see him still watching. *Hmm*, that was unexpected.

Determined to win, she shoved the tail of the shirt down the neckline and then reaching underneath with her hand, tugged it through her bra. The tail rested comfortably just under her breasts and she was now wearing an improvised, but secure, halter top with sleeves. Not a fashion statement, to be sure, but desperate times called for desperate measures.

Besides, that little move had caught Nick's attention. Such a guy! She'd win for sure if she kept this strategy up.

"Come on," the boys whined, anxious for the game to begin. They bounced up and down on the couch in anticipation.

"Okay, I'm ready." She unbuttoned the top of her shorts. Nick sucked in a breath and Amy grinned. "So I'm not so constricted in my movements," she explained. She wanted to laugh out-loud at the pained look on his face. She never imagined the sight of her bellybutton could affect Nick. He'd seen her in a bathing suit hundreds of times over the years.

"Good idea," he said, pulling off his shirt.

Oh, no fair, Amy thought, as her mouth opened and her breathing came in dry little puffs. She'd seen his naked chest before, of course. As many times as he'd seen her bellybutton, if not more. But this time, all that lovely, tanned expanse of skin was bared strictly for her benefit, and she'd be pressing herself against him. A lot.

She reminded herself there was nothing going on here. In fact, she blamed her erotic thoughts on Mr. Horton's revelations, claiming that they'd got her thinking about things she usually tried hard *not* to think about. But that wasn't working. It didn't matter how her thoughts arrived at this place, because she was going to faint, right here, right now.

The little puffs of breath petered out to nothing and her gaze spiraled to a pinpoint focused on Nick's hands moving to his waistband. She knew what he was going to do in response to her suggestive gesture, but it wasn't until he unbuttoned the top of his jeans that she remembered to breath. In a huge gasp. The jeans, which were slung low on his hips to begin with, now dipped lower, revealing boxers and a little more than Amy had seen before, while promising even greater mysteries.

He rolled his shoulders and flexed his chest muscles, rocking his head back and forth in an impressive impersonation of a professional boxer, and Amy clenched her teeth and pulled her gaze up above his shoulders.

"Let's go." He moved into position.

"Wait, let me loosen up, too," Amy said, stalling for time and looking for an advantage. Stretching her arms way over her head, she could feel the bottom of her abbreviated shirt riding up and knew without a doubt that the edge of her lacy pink bra was showing. Not enough to be indecent, but just enough to suggest that it was. Checking Nick's expression, he nodded in her direction, conceding she had indeed made her point. His acknowledgment made Amy feel better and she was able to resume her place in the game.

Balancing on her knees, arms held out in front of her in a defensive pose, she let the cheering from the boys spur her on. They were yelling Nick's name, but that's because like all little boys, they liked to be on the winning team. Little did they know she was going to win. She hadn't quite figured out how yet, but she would.

Nick reached out and grabbed her upper arms, yanked her toward him and as their chests meshed, he flipped her to the side and down. Just like that, she was flat on her back with him grinning at her from above.

She blinked in shock. Okay, maybe she wouldn't win. But by golly, she wasn't giving up this easily. While he hovered over her, waiting for her answering move, she dug her heels into the carpet for traction and abruptly raised her hips into him. Caught off balance, the move provided her with enough room to wiggle free. Breathing heavily from the exertion–*Nick must weigh a ton*–she looked for her chance to get him underneath her.

Unfortunately, he wasn't into the idea of taking turns at being on top. He was coming at her with a menacing grin on his face.

Being on the receiving end of the game actually gave her an advantage because of the adrenaline response it triggered. Excitement sped up her spine and the ancient fight-or-flight instinct rose inside her. Without conscious thought, she threw herself into his chest and wrapped her arms around him; the surprise and the force of the action knocked him on his back, taking her with him.

As Nick toppled over with a whoosh, the boys clapped wildly in disbelief. Pulling her arms out from underneath him, Amy turned her head to smile at them. Jacob gave her a thumbs up. Before she could enjoy that reward, Nick grabbed her ribs and dug his fingers in, wiggling them mercilessly. "You cheat," she managed to get out as she struggled against him. Granted, she was no expert in the sport, but that didn't mean she hadn't watched her share of matches over the years. And in all that time, she'd never once seen one contestant tickle the other.

Finally shaking off his torturing fingers, she spread her full length over his and relaxed into him, effectively pinning him down with her weight. Taking his hands in hers and holding them near his ears, she lifted her torso up and then bent her head, shaking her hair in front of her and draping it over his face.

"You think you got me back there, huh? We'll see about that." She slowly stroked the long strands back and forth over his eyes, nose, and mouth.

As Nick struggled beneath her this time, she gloated in her victory. Deciding he hadn't learned his lesson yet, she leaned down and blew in his ear, then nipped the lobe, her tongue licking the spot immediately afterwards.

Nick froze and Amy raised up in response, to see if she'd

somehow inadvertently hurt him. With his eyes shut she couldn't tell.

"Nick? Are you okay?" Her voice sounded a little breathy to her own ears, but she supposed that was to be expected, given the physical activity that was taking place.

"He's playing dead, Aunt Amy. Don't fall for it." Kevin offered his advice from the sidelines, and she knew he was right. But the possibility of Nick being injured wasn't the problem right now. He still had his eyes shut and his jaw was clenched as tightly as the rest of his body, and Amy was pretty sure she had a good idea why.

From a distance, she heard the boys continue to give her advice, but she couldn't concentrate on what they were saying because she was too busy coming to grips with the realization that her hips were almost even with Nick's. With their bare bellies all but glued to one another, she had a firsthand feel of the steel button of his jeans pressing into her flesh. And that wasn't all that was pressing into her.

No, Nick definitely wasn't playing dead.

Her eyes widened in shock, just about the time he opened his. They stared at each other in uncomfortable silence. She had no idea how to make it stop, or if she even wanted to. The idea that she aroused Nick was so new and so amazing she didn't want to give it up yet, even though it almost killed her to hold his gaze while they each adjusted to this new reality.

"Are you going to finish me off?" Nick asked in a whisper, his eyes staring unflinchingly into hers.

"What?" Amy rasped. His voice was so low she wasn't sure what he'd said. She lowered her gaze to his lips in an attempt to read them when he repeated himself, but they didn't move. His mouth was inches away from hers and slowly her head started to lower. Her vision encompassed only her target and as her whole body relaxed against him, her hands released his. He kept them planted on the floor where they were.

This was it. Do it or die, Amy. If you don't do it, you might just die without ever finding out.

"One, two, three," Jacob counted, jarring Amy's concentration. "Aunt Amy won!"

"*Ew*, they're gonna kiss," Kevin added his observations at almost the same time in a disgusted little boy tone.

"No we're not," Nick said into the silence that followed.

Amy felt her face flame, and Nick's eyebrows formed a confused frown.

The moment was utterly lost and the only hope now was to regain her tattered pride. Was her body really spread, nearly naked, over Nick's? How was she ever going to look at him again? In fact, even now, she forced herself to keep her gaze trained on the pulse in his neck that pounded a rapid rhythm, but that didn't stop her from knowing that Nick's physical response to their situation had been very real. That knowing sent a thrill up her spine that lodged itself at the base of her skull where every hair in the vicinity raised up in awareness. The tingle spread across her shoulders like wildfire to her breasts where her nipples tightened in eager response.

"You won, Amy," Nick said. "You can get off me now."

Still he made no effort to move from under her weight. He was allowing her to call the shots.

"Oh, yeah, right." She thanked God silently that she was wearing a bra. At least her physical response would be masked from him. She hoped.

She jerked herself upright, careful not to dig her knees or elbows into him where he was still in a vulnerable position.

"Although," he continued with a devious smile once she was safely away from him and things were returning to normal. "I want to thank you for the opportunity to experience your...skill."

"Yes, well, let that be a lesson to you," Amy said absently, still not entirely sure what to do with the feelings rampaging through her. Right now she needed to gather all the pieces of herself that had flown off into Kingdom Come while she'd been entertaining unbelievably erotic thoughts about Nick and arrange them in some logical, safe order. The reality of coming this close to her fantasy was almost more than she could bear. Thank goodness the whole thing had only lasted a few minutes and that the boys were too young to realize anything had happened.

On the other hand, was that such a good thing? What would Nick have done if she'd pressed her lips and her hips into him? She'd probably never get the chance to find out.

It was all she could think about as she and the boys savored their ice cream and cookies, while Nick, being a good sport, ate his oatmeal and raisins.

* * *

Son-of-a-bitch.

Rolling over onto his back, Nick folded his hands behind his head and stared into the darkness that obscured the ceiling over his bed. There was no way he was going to get any sleep tonight if he didn't corral his thoughts. The problem was, there was no hope of controlling his thoughts because he'd clearly lost his mind.

It was the only excuse he could come up with to explain his behavior tonight. Not to mention the fact he'd enjoyed his behavior way, way more than he should have. Almost as much as he enjoyed hers.

Thinking back on it yet again, he couldn't pinpoint the exact moment when he'd become aware of Amy as hot. Or desirable. Granted, he'd always thought she was cute, and had even noticed her compact, athletic little body. The curves she'd added recently were nice, too, and if he wanted to be honest, he might as well admit he'd spent a few minutes admiring those curves.

But now, he was downright panting for her, and that scared the crap out of him because he didn't know how it had happened.

When he arrived at the house he wasn't aware she was going to be there, or that she was going to stay. He did immediately notice what she was wearing, but he always did that, so that wasn't anything new or unnerving. Although, come to think of it, he never noticed what Janelle or Ted wore and they were just as much his friends as Amy.

That realization put a wrinkle in his thinking, but surely it didn't mean anything. He frowned, pulling his thoughts away from the pit of self-discovery before he got in too deep, and back to figuring out the events of the evening, including that farce of a wrestling match.

But even the physical challenge had been innocent enough to start. A show for Kevin and Jacob. However, when Amy pulled her shirt up and tucked it into her bra, somehow his thoughts changed from teasing to tortured, just like that he started having thoughts he shouldn't be having, certainly didn't want to be having.

Against his will, his gaze started at her navel and traveled over her smooth, flat stomach, upwards past her ribs, to the little flash of pink satin that peeked out from under the T-shirt's cotton hem. What was revealed wasn't particularly seductive, but that didn't stop his imagination from filling in the sexy details he knew were beneath the flimsy layers of material.

If that hadn't been enough to put him over the top, when she'd unbuttoned her pants…his blood pressure skyrocketed, and his male, predatory interest rose up with awareness. Until he caught a look at her face and realized she was trying to throw him off-guard to give herself an advantage in the match. Which was downright clever of her, and he fell right into the trap, typical man that he was.

Fortunately, his good sense finally came to his rescue and reminded him this was for fun, not for real. So, he decided to fight fire with fire by stripping himself down a notch. When Amy acknowledged she'd received his message, he was able to get his libido under control, comfortable knowing they were once again on safe ground.

Then he touched her bare skin. Fool that he was, he'd somehow forgotten that wrestling involved touching and grappling…and pinning…

Those thoughts were better left alone. The same way he knew he could only be grateful that Kevin and Jacob were present tonight. Otherwise he might embarrass himself by doing something stupid like using his superior strength to roll her underneath him, using his lips to map out her contours, burning them into his mind.

Nick fidgeted and punched his pillow, struggling to restrain his heated imaginings, knowing that where the mind went, the man soon followed. He couldn't follow those thoughts with actions.

So he tried. Again. But it just wasn't working. He sighed in frustration and trained his attention on Kevin and Jacob. That path also led straight to Amy, but from a different, no less alarming, direction. In fact, this one might be even more unnerving because it rested on a variety of domestic visions that scared him more than the erotic ones had.

Visions of Amy on the couch after they settled the boys down, with Jacob in her arms, his head tucked into her shoulder trustingly. Nick had glanced over in time to watch her wrap her arms around Jacob's middle and settle a light kiss on the back of his head.

The subtleties of the moment weren't lost on Nick and longing settled on him, hitting him in the solar plexus, taking his breath. Something was stirring subconsciously, a feeling he didn't understand, almost as though he was missing something vital and had just become aware of the possibility.

He shoved the idea away, more interested in probabilities than possibilities, but the feelings lingered, unsettling and persistent.

In the end, the adults kept the boys up far past their bedtimes, clearly using the children as a buffer between them. Finally, when Jacob was sound asleep in Amy's lap and Kevin about to fall asleep next to Nick, he and Amy each hoisted a child into their arms and carried them off to bed.

Nick had Kevin in bed quickly, the little boy eager to be asleep. Once more Nick placed his hand over the boy's head, wished him peaceful dreams, and quietly left. Kevin was snoring softly before Nick left the room.

He crossed the hall to Jacob's room to find Amy holding the boy in her arms, his little body tucked securely into hers, their fronts pressed tightly together. Jacob was nearly limp and Amy gently swayed back and forth, humming slightly to her precious burden.

He leaned into the doorjamb and waited, the peacefulness of the moment overtaking him, lulling him as it lulled the little boy, making Nick wish for things he normally didn't even think about.

Finally she'd tucked Jacob into his bed and pulled the covers up under his chin. As if reluctant to say a final goodbye, she ran her hand over his forehead and into his hair, smoothing the day away with her touch.

The same rush of emotion Nick experienced earlier as he'd watched Amy tucking in her nephew flooded him now as he lay in bed, and he finally understood what it was.

Impossible though it seemed, he was homesick.

The next day, Nick rang the doorbell for a second time. What was keeping Ted? Checking his watch, he was about to give up when the door opened.

"Hey," Ted said, appearing before Nick. "'Bout time you got here."

"Sorry, tourist season is upon us, with all the traffic that entails," Nick offered up his excuse. An excuse that was understood by every Floridian during the fall/winter months as people descended on the state to wait out the cold weather up north.

Ted ushered him into the house, slapping his back as they walked through the foyer.

"Why is it so quiet around here?" Nick asked.

"Janelle took the kids to a play time at church. The house is all mine for a couple of hours."

Together they went to the back of the house, to Ted's private domain. A little office tucked away in the seclusion of a courtyard.

Once inside, they both fell into worn leather chairs. Nick had been in this room many times over the years, but it never felt stale to him.

Like the rest of the home, the office contained its pair of

potted palms. "Why are there palms all over the house?"

"Janelle likes them," Ted explained. "She says they give the place a tropical feel."

"Well, that's good," Nick said, "Since we live in the tropics."

"I know, go figure." Leaning toward Nick, he lowered his voice, even though the house was empty. "I dump my pencil shavings into them."

Nick laughed conspiratorially, while at the same time noticing the dark greens, reds, and blues, not to mention the floor-to-ceiling bookcase and built-in gaming table the room sported. It truly looked like an old fashioned gentleman's club. Or a smoking room.

Reaching into a desk drawer Ted pulled out two of the biggest cigars he'd ever seen. "One for you," he said. "And one for me. Cheers." He raised his cigar.

Nick saluted, then rolled his cigar in his fingers, testing its tightness, before putting it to his nose for a deep inhale. Smelled like tobacco. Someday, he'd learn the specific protocol for smoking cigars.

Ted bit the end of his cigar off and spit it into the palm tree.

"Won't that hurt the plant?" Nick asked.

"I guess we'll find out," Ted answered, apparently unconcerned. At Nicks' questioning gaze, he relented. "I wouldn't worry. With two kids running loose, and about a year's worth of pencil shavings, these things have so far been tough as Hattie's homemade beef jerky."

That was good enough for him. He bit the end off his cigar and spit it into the plant as well. "What are we celebrating?"

"Oh, this and that." Ted settled deeper into his chair and rested his feet on the ottoman in front of him. "Your new job, for one thing."

He had a glint in his eye that led Nick to believe there was more to this, but he allowed himself to be engaged in conversation. "Yeah, how about that, huh? Did you ever think I'd actually get this close to working with an NFL team?"

Ted shook his head while reaching behind him for a huge cigar lighter. "No, to tell you the truth, I never did. I always figured you'd eventually settle down to your place in life, open your own physical therapy office, get married..." his voice trailed off. "You know, the usual."

He flicked the lighter and leaned back until the flame settled a little before firing the cigar end. He puffed like a pro, even though Nick knew he wasn't.

"Where'd you get the flame thrower?" Nick wanted to know when he was done.

Ted tilted the solid brass lighter and looked at it, squinting one eye against the smoke. "Janelle got it at the flea market. Suppose to be some kind of antique thing specially designed for cigars." He handed it over for his inspection before continuing. "And that means," he said and then waited for Nick to finish the sentence for him.

Nick obliged. "That you have to smoke a few cigars in honor of her gift, right?"

"You got it, my man."

"This thing weighs a ton." Nick tried to get his cigar going.

"Yeah, now, inquiring minds want to know when are you taking off to begin your new position?"

"*Mmm*," he grunted, indicating he'd answer as soon as his cigar was smoking half as good as Ted's. He'd never smoked a cigar before and he was a little surprised at how much work it was.

"There," he said, as he got a little blue curl of smoke going. "I start after Christmas, but before New Year's. They're supposed to contact me with details in the next couple of weeks." He glanced at the tip of his cigar. Shouldn't it be glowing red? He puffed. Nothing.

"You've already given notice at West Coast Rehab?"

He shook his head. "No, I'm using up some vacation time and taking a brief leave of absence, just in case. I want to be ready to go when they need me, but I don't want to burn my bridges quite yet, either."

"That makes sense," Ted agreed, and then went on. "So, I guess all the planning and hard work have finally paid off, huh? You're finally getting what you always wanted most."

He looked up. "Yeah, I guess." Funny, when it was put like that, it didn't seem like such a huge accomplishment. It sounded more like a...sacrifice.

"Oh, by the way," Ted said, a huge grin splitting his face. "Janelle's pregnant again."

"No way!" Nick exclaimed, his cigar and his job forgotten. "Well, ain't you guys figured out what causes that yet?"

Ted laughed. "It's Janelle's fault. I keep having fun, and she keeps taking me seriously."

Ted and Janelle were a family forever couple. Both parents would welcome any children that came along.

"Congratulations, Ted. I mean that. Compared to you guys, my life looks sorta empty." He'd meant that as an encouragement, but realized it was true.

"Nonsense, Nick. Any guy would give his favorite set of golf clubs to have the opportunity you've got knocking on your door."

Nick nodded his head absently. Any guy but Ted.

"So, let's raise our cigars in a toast, shall we? To your new life, may blessings be plenty, and to my life, may I have more blessings than you." He grinned and winked.

"Here, here," Nick echoed, but the toast didn't feel like much of a blessing. Like his cigar, the fire had gone out.

Chapter Five

Amy twisted her fork around in a giant pile of spaghetti, her thoughts and her appetite a million miles away. Still amazed by her resolve to have her "do or die trying" encounter with Nick, she'd been unable to think of anything else.

Well, anything else except what this would do to Michael.

Which brought her back to the present. Sitting across from her, Michael sipped his iced tea and glanced around the stylish Italian restaurant, spaghetti sauce on his chin.

Amy sighed. Nick never got sauce on his chin. He was the only person she knew who could eat spaghetti without even a little bit of a mess. He used both a fork and a spoon, spinning the noodles into one neat bite-sized bale, then popping it in his mouth. Nary a drop of sauce or a smidge of a noodle gone astray.

What was the point of life if you couldn't enjoy a plate of spaghetti without making a bit of a mess? Did everything have to be thought out and accounted for?

She was one to talk. Didn't she account for every little penny?

Yeah, but that was her job. She didn't apply it to every aspect of her life.

That was certainly true. She took the rest of her life as it came, never quite happy, but never unhappy enough to do anything about it.

She twirled the straw in her glass of chocolate milk. "Michael?"

"Yeah?" he said, after slurping up a dangling strand of pasta. The sight urged her on.

"Why do you stay with me? Really?" She had to know. "I mean, I'm not a great cook, not particularly beautiful, there's no…y'know, sex to speak of. What's the attraction?"

He looked at her like she was insane, or like he should be wary of his answer.

"I'm serious," she insisted. "It just doesn't make sense, not in today's society."

He wiped his chin on a red and white checkered napkin. "Well, let's see." He placed the napkin back in his lap and leaned his elbows on the table. Nick didn't do that, either. "You're funny, easy to be with, you don't mind when I slurp my spaghetti."

She supposed all those things were true, but they didn't answer her question.

"Go on," she urged.

He sat there for a few seconds, pondering the question and tapping his chin with his forefinger. "Well, I suppose the main thing is companionship. You really are fun to be with. And besides, you don't complain about my work schedule." He reached across the table and took her hand. "You'd be surprised how many women want you to spend all your time with them, and that really cuts into business hours."

That was probably true. Contrary to what Nick thought, Michael was actually a workaholic, working long hours and frequently bringing work home.

She let him hold her hand while she thought about what he'd said. The more she thought, the less flattering it sounded. He stuck with her because she didn't complain or make demands?

It was worse than she thought. She was utterly passive in her approach to life. Life was happening, while she sat back and watched from a safe distance.

As Michael ran his thumb across the back of her hand, she wondered something else. When the two of them were alone and passionately engaged, how come she never had a problem putting the brakes on?

Was it possible the reason she never made demands on Michael's time was because she just didn't care if he spent it with her or not? And if that was true, what on earth did she care about?

Several things came briefly to mind, but the only one that clamored to be heard was Nick. Always Nick. So, if that was what she cared about, why wasn't she making some demands? Of herself, if not him? She wanted to start living her life, and the first thing she must do was make sure Nick understood exactly what he was leaving behind.

But before she could do that, she'd have to break it to Michael gently that they were through.

Not until she had dessert, though. Changes were great, but this one required a little courage and finesse. And chocolate.

* * *

Forty five minutes later, Amy still didn't know what to say. Two-thirds of a brownie sundae hadn't given her even a bit of courage, and she was suspicious her finesse had gone wandering as well. Here she was, waiting while Michael unlocked the door to her apartment, and still no idea how to tell him.

She could postpone it until later, she supposed. No, it wouldn't get any easier the more she put it off and she really needed this to be over.

Front door standing open, Michael ushered her in. He closed the door with one hand and patted her bottom with the other. Oh yes, she decided as she hung up her purse, it had to be now. "Michael, I need to talk to you about something."

"Okay." He followed her into the living room and sat next to her on the couch.

Amy scooted over to the opposite end, deciding distance was needed to make her announcement clear. She rubbed her palms down her thighs, not sure where to begin.

"I bet I know what this is about," Michael said before she could get started.

"You do?" she said, surprised.

"You want to take our relationship to the next level." He paused.

"Level?" she asked. "What level?"

"Physical level. You know, sex. That's where you were going with that conversation at the restaurant, right?" He stared at her hopefully.

Oh, wow. This was going to be a lot more difficult than she'd thought. Michael was the first guy she'd ever had to break up with. Always before, the men dumped her as soon as they figured out she wasn't kidding when she said no, and they didn't wait around to convince her otherwise.

Except Michael. And she was ready to repay his patience by breaking up with him.

She bit her lip, trying to keep her guilt under control. Her thoughts raced and confusion overwhelmed her. Was this her only option? Choose either Nick or Michael? What if Nick didn't want her? Was it fair, or even wise, to do away with Michael on a risky proposition like this?

On the other hand, could she sneak around trying to seduce

Nick while hoping to hide it from Michael? Wasn't that worse than breaking up with him? And what if she was successful at getting Nick into bed, and then she and Michael did finally end up married? He'd find out for sure she'd been playing games, teasing him all along.

No, it definitely had to be this way. She didn't want to hurt Michael, but she couldn't continue to refuse to take responsibility for her feelings. And sometimes that meant hard choices.

"Okay, Amy, you've gotten so good at playing hard to get you're even doing it in conversation now. Hello? Anyone home?" Michael leaned forward and waved his hand at her.

She brought her gaze to his face and took a deep breath. There was no easy way to do this, so she'd have to just dive in. "Michael, I think we should consider being just friends."

There, she'd done it. Just the way everyone always did it to her. She was proud and relieved. Until she saw his face.

Oh, my. This wasn't going well. He looked angry, not upset. But why?

She held her breath, waiting for his response, but he said nothing. His face hardened and turned cold. He squinted his eyes and clenched his jaw, the muscles throbbing at his temples.

Her stomach clenched in response. Painfully. She was so not good at confrontation. Why wouldn't he say something?

The back of her neck cramped as the muscles of her torso tensed into a knot. Her palms started to sweat and just when she thought she'd shatter from the silence, he spoke.

"Care to give me a reason why?"

She let out her breath in a whoosh. A reason? She couldn't give him a reason. Well, not the real reason. She'd have to come as close to the truth as possible. "I think we should both see other people." There, that was true. Mostly.

"Other people? What other people?"

Oh, boy, now she was sunk. He wasn't letting her off the hook like she thought he would. "Well, nobody specific..." the sentence trailed off, not explaining anything.

"I don't get it," he went on. "You're making absolutely no sense here."

The kicker was, she knew he was right. But she couldn't trust him with her real reasons, not before she had a chance to act on them herself.

"I know this seems irrational, Michael, and I'm sorry. Really. However, I am free to make the decision to see other people if I choose. And so are you. It's not like I'm doing it behind your back."

"Amy, just exactly who else do you think you're going to find willing to put up with your Little Miss Virgin act?"

It was all she could do to keep from cringing. No one had ever said anything this hateful to her. If he was determined to hurt her, he was doing a fine job. And that ticked her off. Who the hell did he think he was? She'd been so worried about his feelings when he seemed to have no concern for hers.

She straightened her shoulders, determined to face him down. "I'm not looking for someone to put up with me. I think that's exactly the point. You put up with my morality, and I put up with your work ethic. There must be more to a relationship than settling. I want to find out. Can't you understand?"

"I understand, all right. I understand you're hot for Nick and probably always have been."

"What does this have to do with Nick?" she asked, astounded he would go there.

"Apparently it's got everything to do with Nick." He stood up and paced in front of her. "I found what you were hiding in your closet. That, plus the way you always watch him, it's obvious."

At her silent shock, he continued. "Your diary, Amy. Come on, let's not pretend here."

"My diary? My high school diary? What in the world are you doing going through my things?" Her mind whirled and her guilt withered in the face of outrage. Where did he get his nerve?

But that was only one question racing through her shocked brain. Questions like "how could he treat her like this?" only made her realize how wrong she'd been about him. He had no respect for her at all.

And if that weren't enough, embarrassment was quickly filling in the places where anger that surged only a moment before was now ebbing. What else had he pawed through? Her underwear drawer? Did he try on her shoes? Maybe take a bubble bath and use her loofah? The possibilities were endless, and sickening.

For a woman with a placid temperament, these quick mood changes were breathtaking.

"I was wondering what you didn't want me to see in that box. Seems you did have a little secret after all."

"That's ancient history, Michael."

"Is it?" he countered.

She put her hand to her forehead. This was too much. She couldn't decide where to go from here in the conversation. Should she deny her feelings? Maintain her horror that Michael had spied on her? Comfort him and tell him her rejection had nothing to do with Nick?

Michael faced no such dilemma. "He's not going to deal with your prudishness any better than I did. He'll eventually find someone to spend his *quality* time with, same as I did."

Amy's hand fell away and she was certain her mouth was hanging open. Could this get any worse? Was everything she believed a lie? She tried to wrap her brain around the fact that she didn't know Michael at all. He had manipulated her, lied to her, made her believe he cared, for God's sake.

But he wasn't done enlightening her to his escapades. "It's true," he said, standing in front of her, stiff and unyielding. "I have never been faithful to you. No one ever could. It's ridiculous and unnatural to think anyone would."

"I don't understand," she mumbled. All she wanted was a straightforward parting of the ways. Why all the disillusionment? Why did he have to humiliate her this way?

He shrugged. "I wanted to be associated with Gilbert Homes."

Amy shook her head. "But, we're not rich. You wouldn't get any money from dating, or even marrying me."

"Not money," Michael agreed. "Prestige. Your family name and reputation is all but legendary in this town. You're practically founders, for heaven's sake. It would be a nice little boost to my resume to be tied to such upstanding citizens."

"So, you weren't really working all the time like you said? You were using me to build your business?"

Michael's careless shrug emphasized his cold-blooded plan. "It seemed doable at the time. And when I started it, I hoped for a loving future with you. But, I met someone else shortly after. She's demanding and, shall we say, affectionate. Most of the things you're not. Too bad she lacks your pedigree."

That explained a lot of Michael's behavior, Amy realized, but not why he'd give up so easily. She asked him.

"Because you weren't paying off like I figured you would. I

thought tonight would be my lucky night, but turns out it's time to cut my losses instead. So be it."

He headed to the door, pausing on his way out for one last shot. "I hope you're happy with your life, Amy. This is the bed you've made; you'll have to lie in it. Too bad you're going to be all alone when Nick goes off to play touch-and-feel with the cheerleaders."

And with that he was gone, taking all the air out of the room with him as he went.

For one brief moment, Amy was livid. Not with Michael, although he certainly earned it. No, she was upset and disappointed in herself. Why was she such a dishrag that she just let him say those things, do those things, with very little repercussions from her? Couldn't she stand up for herself at all? Was she completely spineless?

As she sat on the couch, trying to understand what it was she'd done wrong, it wasn't until she'd wracked her brain and gotten a headache that it occurred to her she wasn't responsible for this. She hadn't gone through his things, she hadn't cheated on him. Not really. She had every right in the world to break up with him if she wanted to, even though her motives weren't particularly pristine, they were honest. All she wanted was to be responsible for her life and feelings and if he didn't like it, that was his problem.

And frankly, she was downright lucky to get away!

It wasn't until she'd come this far in her reasoning that she also decided to let herself off the hook because she hadn't ranted back at him as he deserved. In fact, she was proud of herself for taking the high road, setting an example of maturity instead of resorting to juvenile name-calling and tantrums.

She picked at the piping on a cushion while she gave herself the pep talk. The piping was coming loose before she had herself completely convinced, but it was a worthwhile sacrifice.

Chapter Six

A few days later, Nick bounced along in the passenger's seat of the miniscule SUV, all the while trying to come up with a way to escape the clutches of the kidnappers who held him captive.

The wind from the open window rushed past his head, competing with the thumping stereo, and making it impossible for him to discern what his captors were saying, although he noticed they didn't seem to have any problem conversing. In fact, with their heads close together, they appeared to be laughing gaily, probably at his expense as they plotted his eventual demise. He wished the person driving would look straight ahead.

Checking the dashboard, he breathed a little easier seeing the passenger side air bag. Alone in his thoughts, isolated from the others, he tugged at the seatbelt where it dug into the side of his neck. The gesture made him appreciate the adjustable belts in his sedan.

Closing his eyes, he gave in to the headache that kept time to the beat blaring from the speakers. So far tonight they'd hit three bars and were on their way to the fourth and–please, God–final one.

How did he get into this mess? He thought back over his day, attempting to see where he'd gone so horribly wrong. The images rolled through his brain in quick succession, photo-album style.

The impromptu trip had thrown him a bit, but he said he'd make himself available and so he had.

Once settled at his hotel, he set off on his own, arriving at the complex for a morning full of meetings. The whole reason he was here was a meet-and-greet, designed to give him a chance to settle in a bit before the new job began.

Determined to make a good impression, he took notes, not trusting his brain to record all the information coming at him. Lunch consisted of a sandwich, heavy on the mustard, and more talk of his duties once he took over the rehabilitation of the cheerleaders.

And speaking of cheerleaders, that's where his memory became hazy. He vaguely recalled meeting them all while they practiced for an upcoming game. It wasn't long before his libido was dizzy from being surrounded by so much flexible female flesh. Throughout the conversation, he'd worked hard to keep from sounding like a dork.

After a while, the ladies trickled away, one by one, until only Sandy, Mandy, and Jane remained. The group of four chatted for a while, and then Jane suggested the three of them take him out on the town before he left tomorrow.

His already testosterone-fuzzy brain went blank while his male instincts went on high alert. Gone were any thoughts of getting some sleep before his first-thing-in-the-morning flight home. Somehow, the thought of being outnumbered three to one by beautiful women seemed a dream come true.

Now, as they tortured him through the night, that dream had long since passed nightmare status.

"Here we are," Mandy said from the back seat.

Nick jumped in response, wincing from the strangling hold of the seatbelt and marveling at how her loud, rah-rah voice managed to overcome the booming speakers. Definitely impressive.

Jane turned down the radio and Mandy continued, her voice not adjusted to the semi-silence. "This is the hottest club in town. We saved the best for last," she assured him.

"Great," he said, his lack of enthusiasm going unnoticed. If he ever got home alive, he swore on a stack of Sports Illustrated magazines he'd never complain about the lack of nightlife again.

As the three girls bounded out of the vehicle, he seriously regretted his bout of ego-induced stupidity. It didn't help that while he was dragging his tail the three girls seemed to be as energetic as they'd been six hours earlier. Which was probably why they were the cheerleaders and he wasn't.

Glancing at the building outlined in green neon, he reeled back at the line of people snaking around the corner. "Are all those people waiting to get in?" He couldn't believe it, it was almost midnight on a Wednesday night. Didn't any of them have to work tomorrow? Where he came from, Saturday night wasn't this happening.

"Yeah," Mandy, the loud one, yelled. Nick was getting used to it, and he wondered why he hadn't noticed it earlier in the day. "Told you this place was hot!"

Sandy, the quiet one, grabbed his hand. "Don't worry," she said. "We know the owner. We won't have to wait."

She tugged, but he dug in his heels. He had to give himself this chance at freedom. "Why don't you guys just run me back to the hotel and I'll crash there for a while?"

He could tell by their faces it wasn't happening.

"Don't be silly," Jane, the sensible one, said. "We want you to have a good time, not go back to Florida telling everyone how boring we are up here."

That's when he realized he was trapped. Trapped like a cat with three very charming and determined mice who held him hostage in a strange town. No, not mice. Canaries. Three bright, frenetic, chirping canaries fluttering about his head, clogging his senses with promises he couldn't even remember.

He shook himself free of the image. "Maybe we should wait our turn, like everyone else." It seemed a reasonable suggestion to him.

Mandy turned around. "Are you crazy? We'd never get in if we got in line. Trust me, we do this all the time."

Squelching his groan, he gave in gracefully, trying not to notice the glares coming his way as they headed to the front of the line. Those people would just have to understand he was too weak from lack of sleep to fight.

Standing at the door while the three ladies paid their cover, Nick was surprised to feel the music vibrating from the sidewalk up through his shoes. Yeah, this was going to be fun.

Peeking behind him, he wondered if he could make a break for it. One look at the physical fitness of his kidnappers and he knew they'd be on him before he cleared the parking lot.

Now, if he weren't exhausted, he'd give them a run for their money, but right this minute, there was no way.

He briefly considered appealing to the patrons standing in line, but who would believe he was being forced to party against his will?

He gave up, paid his cover, and followed Sandy into the bar. Maybe the three of them would all head to the bathroom at once and he could just stroll out, unnoticed.

Upon entering, whirling lights took his breath and his balance as pinpoints of color bounced off every surface. His headache roared to life, the flashes taking the pain to a new level.

Shielding his eyes from the onslaught, he nonetheless proceeded further into the din. Fortunately, once past the very front, the lighting became less hostile and his headache settled to a dull throb. Track lighting emphasized specific areas, such as dance floor and bar.

The place was jumping. There were literally people wall-to-wall, and he worried about fire safety. How would all these people get out in the event of an emergency? No doubt about it, he would memorize where the red exit signs were located.

Packed together like they were, there was very little breathing room. In his younger days, he would've been grateful for the innocent chance to brush up against beautiful women, but now, he felt claustrophobic.

Turning his head, he searched behind him for a way out, but the sea of night owls had closed in around him and no sign of an escape route was visible. There was no choice, and he followed the girls as they made a sharp left turn, stopping abruptly when he realized they were headed to the dance floor.

No way. No matter what they said or did to him, no matter how they smiled or tilted their heads his way, he wasn't going out there. He leaned down, yelling into Jane's ear. "I'm going to get a beer, do you want anything?"

She smiled, shook her head, and gyrated her hips in a most impressive display. Clearly she was capable of walking and chewing gum at the same time. And more.

He tore his gaze away and looked for the others, to ask if he could get them something, but they were gone, vanished into the mist rising off the floor. Jane soon followed and Nick was left alone to find his way back to the bar.

Finally, beer in hand, he settled in for the long haul, and while his three energizer buddies laughed and danced and had a great time, he spent the next ninety minutes holding up a wall with his back, wondering why bars had to be so crowded and noisy and full of cigarette smoke.

And when the hell did he get so old he noticed those things?

* * *

Inserting the key into the lock, Amy congratulated herself for her genius. A quick peek around the corner assured her the house was deserted. Still, it made her nervous to sneak into someone's home with such a daring scheme.

Not that she was technically sneaking. Nick was out of town, meeting with officials from the team to go over some procedural stuff. Before he left, she'd wrangled a spare key from him, reasoning that in the event of an emergency someone should be able to get into his house.

No emergency came to mind when he asked her for one, but nonetheless, he gave her a spare and thanked her for her concern. She smirked at her guile. Where it came from she wasn't sure, but it came in handy in her quest to bring Nick down.

The thought occurred to her that she was no better than Michael, but she reasoned she didn't intend to go through Nick's things, or keep the key indefinitely. As soon as he came home she'd return it to him. Still, the thought nagged at her and followed her through the door. She promised herself she would never do this again.

Once inside, she pocketed the key and stepped into the living room. While she was here, she might as well look around, just in case something needed her attention.

A quick inspection of the front rooms showed nothing out of the ordinary, so she headed to the kitchen. Setting her purse on the counter, she took a plastic tumbler from the cupboard and gave it a quick sniff, because you just never knew with bachelors whether they could properly load a dishwasher or not.

When it checked clear of sour odors, she grabbed a handful of ice from the fridge, dropped it into the plastic tumbler, and checking the expiration date on the carton, poured herself a glass of milk. As she took the initial sip, she was glad no one was nearby to point out how weird milk on-the-rocks was.

Clinking sounds filled the air as she swirled the ice in the glass, and she let her gaze wander around the room. She raised an eyebrow when she noticed the light on his answering machine flashing. Mesmerized, she debated whether she should check his messages, trying to convince herself it could be something vitally important he needed to be made aware of.

In the end, she rationalized that Nick would be home tomorrow. Anything that was on there could wait that long.

Speaking of which, she needed to get moving. Taking one final sip, she eyed the remainder of the drink, deciding that, as usual, she'd poured too much and wouldn't be able to finish. Moving to the sink to dump it out, she held the glass lightly between two fingers. Still thinking about the answering machine she wasn't paying attention as the bottom of the glass caught on the very edge of the countertop.

With a mind of its own, the tumbler spun out of her hand and plummeted to the ceramic tile floor, spinning end over end.

Upon impact, it bounced into the air once more, unwilling to settle down peacefully on the floor, spraying what was left in the glass into the air in an impressive, somewhat artistic display, covering everything in sight with a sprinkling of white drops.

Shock held her still as the glass finished its damage, until finally it rolled over to where she stood, bumping into her toe. Surveying the mess, Amy ground her teeth in an effort to keep from cussing a blue streak. What difference would it make, since no one was around to hear? Still, she knew that losing her temper wasn't going to make anything better, so she added counting to ten to the teeth grinding, and by the time she reached twelve, she found herself over the upset.

Now to clean up the mess.

She scanned the countertop for paper towels, finding only an empty cardboard tube sitting next to the sink. Great.

A quick check of the cupboards didn't reveal any replacements, so she decided to grab a mop.

She checked the laundry room, turning up nothing there but a rather large pile of dirty laundry. Now what was she supposed to do? No paper towels, no mop, and it wasn't like you could let milk air-dry like you could water.

Spying several bath towels in the clothes mountain, she figured they would have to do. Grabbing two to start, she made her way back to the kitchen.

Working quickly, she was done with the mess in no time. She tossed a load of laundry in the washer, towels included and moved on.

Grabbing her purse from the kitchen counter, she looked it over for milk spots. Not seeing any, she held it by the strap and headed to Nick's bedroom.

Once inside she opened the blinds, letting in some light and dispelling the feeling that she was sneaking around. Hands on hips she surveyed the room, supremely unimpressed. A queen-sized bed with a plaid comforter, an overstuffed chair with coordinating throw pillow, and a TV perched on a large dresser. That was the total ambiance of Nick's bedroom.

Nothing extra, nothing remotely personal. As if he didn't really live here. He only passed time until something better came along.

The thought sent chills along her spine, reminding her that was why she was here, because he did have something better coming along.

Not wanting to waste any more time than necessary, she hustled over to the bed. Picking up a pillow, she buried her nose in it, breathing in the clean, masculine smell that belonged to Nick. She fluffed it gently, then paused, listening. It almost sounded like someone shutting a car door.

Her heart pounding in her throat, she took the pillow with her to the window and peered out, only to see a woman across the street pulling groceries from her car. Reassured it wasn't Nick coming home early, Amy went back to the bed, fluffing the pillow again as she went.

Setting it back down on the bed, she reached into her purse and pulled out a bottle of spray perfume. A perfume she wore all the time. Smiling secretly to herself she picked up the pillow and sprayed it front and back. Throwing the bottle onto the rumpled comforter, she picked up the other pillow, fluffed it, then sprayed it as well.

There. By the time he laid down on them the scent would have mellowed to the point that it brought her gently to his mind.

Placing them back in their places at the head of the bed, she took a few seconds to pull the sheets and comforter up. Armed with the bottle of perfume, she entered his bathroom. She flipped the light switch and looked around, her head tilted to the side, contemplating whether or not to spray the bath towels hanging uniformly from the bar.

She shook her head, deciding she wanted him thinking of her when he was in bed, not when he was in the shower.

That settled, she replaced the cap and stuck the perfume back into her purse. She moved to the sink and washed her hands quickly, noticing the roll of paper towels hanging innocently under the mirror. Grabbing a handful, she dried her hands, refusing to dwell on the fact that if she'd just checked the bathroom earlier she could've saved herself a great deal of work in the kitchen. The whole episode was over. There was no use crying over spilt milk. Literally.

She turned her attention back to her mission, and after congratulating herself in the mirror for a job well done, she gave herself a mental pat on the back and left the room, content that her scent now mingled on the pillows with Nick's. All that was left to do was toss the laundry into the dryer when the timer went off, and her mission was accomplished.

Stopping in the kitchen for one more task, she penned a quick note to Nick, explaining the spill and the clean clothes. The washer beeped that its cycles were complete just as she signed her name, and once the dryer was whirring, she left the house, excitement thrilling throughout her body at the thought of what she'd done.

* * *

Exhausted, Nick made his way through the front door of his house. Dropping his bags, he headed for the kitchen, exactly two things on his mind. A tall glass of orange juice and then a long nap. It wasn't until this very second that he decided in which order he was going to have them.

Pouring the juice he had the drink halfway gone before he noticed the note on the counter top. Even before seeing the handwriting he knew it had to be from Amy. Nobody else had access while he was gone.

He tried to ignore the paper, knowing if it were something important she would've called him, but in the end, he figured there wasn't much energy involved in simply reading what she had to say.

Dear Nick, this is just to let you know that everything around the place is fine, but I wanted to tell you that I spilled a glass of milk while I was here. Unfortunately, it was quite a bit of milk.

I soaked up the puddle, wiped the mess up, and mopped the floor with bath towels because I couldn't find paper ones or a mop. When I put them in the laundry room, I noticed a pile of dirty clothes sitting there, so I tossed a load in the washer. It's in the dryer still, probably very wrinkled, but you'll just have to deal with that. I draw the line at ironing.

Ironing? Nick frowned. He never ironed his clothes. Funny, as particular as he was about things, clothes didn't make the list. Probably because growing up he never had the designer stuff to worry about, so he never learned to fuss over them. Still, maybe he should look into getting an iron, in honor of his new job and subsequent life. Rolling the stiffness from his shoulders, he continued with the note, scanning it quickly to find his place.

Blah, blah, blah...

I draw the line at ironing. Besides, I checked and you don't have an iron. How do you get dressed in the morning?

Anyway, I just wanted you to know you owe me for doing your laundry. Hope you had a great trip.
—Amy

Once he finished, Nick crumpled the note, too tired to worry about mopping and ironing and spilled milk. He just wanted to study the insides of his eyelids for about three hours.

He rinsed the glass, placing it in the sink, and then

staggered across the room. Through the doorway, around the corner, and down the hall, the door to his bedroom was in sight, and before he knew it he was passing through it.

And there–finally!–was his bed, all made up nice and tidy. Apparently Amy felt him inept in this area too, since he just drew the covers up each morning.

Collapsing onto the mattress, he groaned in relief. To be flat on his back was such a reward after the past twenty-four hours. He remembered days gone by when sleep hadn't been such a priority, but it seemed those days were becoming more and more distant.

Kicking off one shoe, then the other, he rolled over onto his stomach, burying his face in the pillow, breathing in deep, and then releasing it in a sigh. The tension slowly eased as he soaked in the soft scent emanating from his pillowcases.

Amy must've changed his sheets as well, because he sure didn't recall them smelling so fresh before he left. He'd have to remember to thank her. She was such a nice person. She probably wouldn't take an unsuspecting guy out on the town, dragging him here and there and everywhere until he couldn't see straight from exhaustion.

He liked that about her.

He also liked that she didn't talk loud. That was a plus. He would like to see if she could do that smiling, tilting, gyrating thing, though.

Turning his head to the side, he sprawled his arms and legs, taking up as much of the bed as possible, but try as he might, sleep eluded him. Most likely he was still wired from the trip, which was inconvenient as hell.

Flopping over onto his back, he punched the pillows a couple of times, smiling as the subtle scent surrounded him. He wasn't used to domesticity. It was only recently he learned to load a dishwasher properly, and Amy was right, laundry was almost beyond him. So, he avoided it by waiting until everything he owned was dirty, thereby making the chore far more onerous than it had to be. So far, he hadn't done a thing to change the behavior.

Speaking of behavior, what was wrong with him? One day he was the playboy of his hometown, and a birthday or two later, he was drinking his beer from a glass. It didn't make sense.

And if that didn't confuse him, the cheerleaders had him truly baffled. He was out on the town with three gorgeous, young, exciting women, and all he could think about was getting home? It was almost as if he were somehow thrown off by the situation. The lack of control, loss of familiarity, or something.

Not that the ladies in question seemed put off by him. They'd been determined to force him to have a good time, but the harder they tried, the less fun he had.

He felt the frown that creased his brow. The whole thing didn't make sense. This job might not *be* everything he wanted, but it led *to* everything he wanted.

So he should've looked at the whole party situation in the light of opportunity. But he hadn't been able to shake the feeling that it was actually keeping him from what he really wanted. That the harder he tried to force his happiness, the less happy he became.

Although, the truth was, if he wanted to leave so badly, all he had to do was walk out the door. They hadn't actually been keeping him hostage.

So why hadn't he done that? Clearly he wasn't interested in partying the night away, so why didn't he do something about it?

One by one his IQ points were slipping into slumber,

making it difficult to concentrate and impossible to actually think. A jaw-cracking yawn stifled his weary attempts at self-discovery, and as he finally slipped into unconsciousness, he decided to get Amy a thank-you gift for watching his house.

He wondered what kind of perfume she wore.

* * *

Bleary-eyed from lack of sleep, Nick slogged his way through the mall packed with Christmas shoppers. Most of his gifts were already bought, but he was determined to get a gift for Amy.

Damned if he knew what to get her, though.

But it wasn't from a lack of options. Everywhere he looked there was a stunning array of items to blow your money on. The display boggled the mind and he'd already spent a great deal of time perusing the wares.

So far, he was torn between a dancing red and green palm tree with fuzzy purple coconuts, and a laminated purse made out of recycled newspapers. The palm was a gag gift, of course, but one he was sure Amy would find amusing.

The little dancing tree must have a motion detector in it because whenever anyone got close to it, the tree started swaying while singing "Let it Snow." In fact, Nick was so amused by it that it wasn't until the third time he watched the performance he noticed the front of the tree had a mouth and sunglasses. Apparently he was standing behind the tree without knowing it.

Anyway, cute as that was, he figured the newspaper purse was more practical. Picking one up, he read the news from over a year ago, and had to admit it was a clever recycling job, although he wasn't sure how sturdy it was. Opening it up for a peek inside, he wasn't impressed by what he saw. It looked exactly like the inside of any purse he'd ever seen. There wasn't a single special feature on the inside. And they wanted a fortune for it. The dancing and singing palm was looking better.

He set the purse down and rubbed his chin, unable to decide.

And that's when it hit him. That smell. It wafted into his awareness, reminding him of something he couldn't quite get hold of. He looked up, took another sniff, paused, sniffed again, turning his head to the left. Sure enough, the tantalizing odor seemed to be coming from an attractive brunette in a mini skirt and platform boots standing to the side of him, a baby on her hip.

Needing to be sure, he leaned nonchalantly in her direction, trying to cop another undetected whiff. But the baby was on to him. Without a single gurgle or squeal of warning, he reached out a pudgy fist and grabbed a handful of Nick's hair. Then he tugged with all his baby might.

"*Yeow*," Nick yelled, but the baby held firm, leaving Nick bent over at the waist and leaning at an alarming angle toward the young mother, a captive of the intrepid infant. If the situation itself weren't bad enough, the baby's ecstatic giggles ensured that everyone around them turned to see what had him so happy.

"Aaron, no!" The mother finally took control. By her voice, Nick gathered she was almost as embarrassed as he was. She tried to disentangle him from her baby's death grip, peeling his fingers free one at a time. "I am so sorry! He's gotten so grabby lately. I should have him in a stroller, but the poor little guy's going through separation anxiety and hates for me to put him down. I'm sure you understand."

Nick nodded his head, free at last, even though he had no clue what "separation anxiety" was.

"Oh, dear," the woman said, reaching into the diaper bag

hanging at her side. "I'm afraid you've got baby spit all in your hair in that one spot. Here, let me get that for you." Standing on her toes, she used the hand containing the handi-wipe to pull Nick's head toward her, with a much gentler touch than her son had. She rubbed at his hair with the wipe using one hand, putting her body between him and Grabby Boy.

"There," she said when she was done crumpling the wipe into a ball and stuffing it back into the bag. "Good as new. Well, except it's still wet and sticky, but now it smells like baby powder." She grinned at him. "I'm so sorry."

Nick was more embarrassed than hurt. "It's okay, no harm done." He rubbed the tingling on his head. She was right, it was wet and sticky. He refrained from raising his fingers to his nose to see if he indeed smelled like baby powder, saying instead, "He's a strong little boy."

"Yes, he is," the mother agreed with a proud grin. An extended pause ensued before the woman finally put an end to it. "Well, anyway, Merry Christmas!" and with that she turned to walk away.

The action reminded Nick how this whole situation had begun. "Wait!" he said abruptly, much to his own surprise, taking an impulsive step toward her.

She turned, her head tilted in inquiry. "Yes?"

Normally he would feel awkward doing this, but they were sorta introduced now, so he plunged ahead. "I hope you don't think this is strange, but I wondered if I could ask you something?"

"Sure," she responded. "Ask me anything."

"Well, it's your perfume. I wonder if you wouldn't mind telling me the name of it? For a friend of mine." For the first time, Nick was glad that baby Aaron had accosted him. It made his request now seem less like a come-on, and he was grateful, sticky hair and all.

"Sure," she said again. "Ask Me Anything."

Nick frowned, wondering if perhaps her son hadn't pulled her hair too hard a time or two. "Okay," he said, cautiously, enunciating the words one syllable at a time, as though the hair pulling could've affected her hearing. "Could you tell me the name of your perfume?"

"Yes," she laughed, enjoying some private joke. "It's called Ask Me Anything."

The light went on, much to Nick's relief. The day was becoming a study in weird. "Oh, I get it," Nick said, but simply knowing the name didn't solve his problem. "Do you happen to know where I can get some?" At her raised eyebrows, he quickly assured her, again, that it was for a friend of his.

She nodded her head over her left shoulder. "Try that department store over there. Just ask at the cosmetic counters, they'll know how to help you."

"Thanks," Nick said, but she was already on her way.

Glancing at his watch he figured he had enough time to hit the store and still be back in time to check ESPN for the continuous sports updates.

Chapter Seven

Making his way to the counter like a man who bought women's perfume every day, Nick waited patiently for the redheaded sales clerk to notice him. When she finally did, he gave her his most engaging grin. He was feeling festive and he wanted to make her job a little more pleasant if he could. A positive attitude was a good place to start.

"Yes, Sir," she acknowledged him, her penciled on eyebrows giving her a surprised look. "May I help you?"

"You certainly may," Nick said, rapping his knuckles on the glass. "Ask Me Anything."

The woman placed her hand to her chest and reared back slightly. "I beg your pardon?"

"It's okay…" Nick checked her nametag quickly. "Muriel. This may be my first time, but I know what I'm doing. Ask Me Anything."

"Well, all right," Muriel agreed, skeptically, then took a few seconds to look him carefully up and down. "Boxers or briefs?" She stared him straight in the eye as she said it.

It was Nick's turn to be taken aback. Then he realized she was only accommodating what he'd said. He'd been trying so hard to be friendly, he'd forgotten to guard against being stupid.

"Sorry, Muriel. I'm looking for the perfume, *Ask Me Anything*." He waited for her to understand.

"*Oh*." She perked up at the opportunity for a sale. "Why

didn't you say so?"

He refrained from reminding her that he had. "Sorry. Do you have any?"

"Well, as a matter of fact, this is your lucky day. Not only do I have it available, but I have it in three different sizes, depending on your needs."

His needs were minimal; he'd better start there. "I'll take the small bottle, thanks." As he waited for her to get it for him he noticed the mirrored tray containing samples to his right. Tilting the bottles this way and that to read their labels, he found the Ask Me Anything sample and sprayed it. Its scent soon filled the air and he found himself hoping Amy liked his choice. But what if she didn't?

Maybe he should get her a gift certificate and let her choose her own present.

The thought held merit, and he was almost ready to tell Muriel he'd made a mistake, when she returned to the counter, the small bottle in one hand, and the medium-sized one in the other. Nick frowned, but Muriel was undaunted.

"Now," she began. "If you buy the small bottle today, you receive this lovely little manicure set that clips onto a key-chain as a free gift." She reached beneath the counter and he heard her feeling around, the rustling paper a dead giveaway. Finally, she pulled something out and set it on the counter in front of him. "It looks a little like a Swiss army knife, doesn't it?"

Nick nodded. Taking the contraption into his hands, he first squeezed the nail clippers. Sure enough, they worked. With very little effort, he pulled out first the nail file, then a pair of tweezers, and something he didn't recognize. "What's this?"

"That's the buffer, to get that healthy shine on your nails." She took the key-chain by the buffer and grabbed his hand, rubbing his thumbnail repeatedly, generating quite a bit of heat. He was about ready to pull away in discomfort when she stopped and leaned back. "There," she said.

"Oh," Nick said, looking at his thumb. The nail did have a shine to it now that wasn't there before. He wasn't sure why he needed shiny nails, or when he'd ever use the buffer, but it was kinda cool. Maybe he'd give the little set to Amy as well as the perfume.

He was just about to tell Muriel he was sold, and then she pulled something else out from her stash under the counter.

"Now," she began again, her eyelashes beating fast enough to create a breeze. "If you buy the next size up, the medium bottle, you'll receive the manicure set and this lovely bath set, containing shampoo, conditioner, loofah mitt and," she paused, reaching for the last item in the little wicker basket.

"Is that a soap-on-a-rope?" Nick interrupted.

"Yes, it is," Muriel confirmed with glee.

"I used to love that stuff!" He looked suspiciously at the bottles. "Can I smell the shampoo?"

She handed him the bottle. He spun the top off and inhaled, deciding that the nutty smell didn't strike him as too girly after all. "Okay, I'll take the medium-sized bottle." The freebies would save him a trip to the store for hair care products later this week.

"Now, hold on." She stopped his runaway sales train. "You should at least consider the large-sized bottle."

He stiffened. This was going a little too far. What did she think he was, a pushover? He'd hold his ground. The medium-sized bottle was as far as he was going.

Until he saw the Holy Grail of giveaways. "Now," Muriel said, and he knew he was a goner. "If you buy the large sized bottle, you get the manicure set, the bath set, and this sturdy, reinforced, specially formulated plastic, tackle-style jewelry case, plus the travel-anywhere umbrella in either solid hunter green, navy blue, or this plaid combining both."

"Whoa," he breathed. The tackle box would hold a lot of screws and bolts, not to mention wire ties and drill bits. Plus it was small enough to fit into a drawer in his kitchen, so he wouldn't have to run to the garage every time he needed something. He'd never bothered with an umbrella before, but he supposed a complimentary one wouldn't be so bad.

Nick had no idea women were getting all this free stuff every time they shopped. He always got his cologne at the drugstore and nobody gave him anything. Clearly, he was seriously missing out, but that was about to change. "Okay, Muriel, you got me. I'll take the big bottle, but that's as far as I'm going." A guy had to have limits, after all.

"Oh, don't worry, young man," she said with a smile. "That's the biggest bottle we have. But if you come back next year, maybe that'll be changed. For sure the gifts will be." She started singing "Let it Snow" under her breath as she bagged up his goods, reminding Nick of the little palm tree he was looking at earlier. This perfume purchase was definitely the smarter way to go.

He watched her ring him up and as she ran his credit card through the system, he noticed some fancy, flowered gift boxes sitting on the floor in an intricate display. "How do I get one of those?" he asked, suspicious that she was holding out on him.

"You have to earn them," she said over her shoulder absently.

"Oh. How do I earn one?" He didn't get it–they were just boxes after all.

"You must buy twenty-five dollars worth of product," she said without glancing his way.

"Did I buy twenty-five dollars worth of stuff?" He wanted to know, because that box would come in handy. If he stuck a bow on top, he could consider the gift wrapped.

Returning to stand before him, she said, "Sir, you've got five boxes coming."

Nick breathed deep in satisfaction at scoring five boxes, then choked when he did the math. "Five?" How could one bottle of perfume wrack up five of those boxes?

"Yes, sir, five. But just remember all the free stuff you got, too!" She grinned at him as she handed him back his credit card along with the receipt to sign.

While he penned his signature, he repeated her words silently to himself. "Remember all the free stuff, remember all the free stuff." Strangely enough, it helped, even though he knew none of it was really free.

Grabbing his bags he turned to leave, determined to get away before she started showing him some "free" power tools.

"Just one more thing, if you please." Muriel stopped him in his tracks.

What now? He turned and waited, afraid to look. "Yes?"

She winked conspiratorially. "You forgot to answer me. Boxers or briefs?"

Amy fastened the final button at her throat and gave up on the day, just as her doorbell chimed.

Suppressing a groan of frustration, she glanced quickly into the mirror, debating whether or not she should change into something more presentable.

Hang it, she decided. She didn't have the energy. Her day

at work had been chaotic with several building code issues having to be addressed. Ted wasn't in the office, so that left her to deal with subcontractors and county officials, all because the residential designer neglected to properly designate electrical outlets. Those impacted other installations and she had to do her best to calm her clients, the homeowners, who didn't understand what the big deal was.

Besides that, her emotions were in a jumble over what she'd done to get Nick's attention and now someone was probably going to try to sell her a subscription to a magazine no one had ever heard of.

It was too much. All she wanted right now was dinner and a good night's sleep. There was a pot of chili bubbling on the stove and a box of corn muffins waiting to be mixed up. Whoever was at the door was just going to have to deal with her flannel Scooby-Doo pajamas and her cranky attitude.

She scuffed to the front of her apartment, the attached feet of the jammies making scratchy sounds on the tile as she went. Peeking through the peephole, she hissed in surprise, wishing she hadn't been so hasty in deciding to remain dressed for bed.

Patting her hair back a little, hoping it wasn't as flyaway as it felt, she opened the door. "Nick! What are you doing here?" She hoped her nervousness would be mistaken as surprise.

"I come bearing gifts," he answered, and as he stepped inside he indicated a large, rectangular box. It was beautifully patterned with poinsettias covering every square inch, some in red, some in pink, others in white. There were even a few of the so-called purple ones she saw for sale in the grocery stores, although she thought they were more pink than purple. Still, it was an interesting variation.

The light-handed embossing of gold added a formality to

the present's festive appearance, as did the large gold bow and trailing red and gold streamers. As a whole, the package was stunning. Which very likely explained why Amy was stunned.

"Isn't it a little early for Christmas?" she wondered aloud. "I don't even remember which closet I put your presents in." Exchanging holiday gifts was the only explanation she could come up with to explain why he would show up at her door without calling. It certainly beat the heck out of her initial panic-laden idea that he'd come to confront her about his bed!

He handed her the package and took his coat off, hanging it on the hall tree while she stared at him, waiting for an explanation. It wasn't long in coming. "I wanted to get you something. To thank you for checking on my house while I was out of town."

His thoughtfulness was completely unexpected, but her response wasn't.

She blushed. Not that there was anything unusual about a person blushing over an expressed appreciation, but in this case, his gift enhanced Amy's guilt over her act of insinuating herself into his dreams and thoughts. Curse her overactive conscience anyway.

"You didn't have to do that!" And she meant it. "Really." Just in case he didn't believe her.

"I know that," Nick said with a happy grin. "I didn't say I had to get you something. I said I wanted to. Big difference."

Ducking her head, she turned the box over in her hands to cover her discomfort.

Get over yourself, Amy. The man brought you a simple present, not the crown jewels. Let him be nice, for pity's sake.

The pep talk had its effect and she was soon leading him into the living room. Settling on the couch, she waited until he seated next to her before peeling open the gift. She had to admit, she was curious what the box contained. And although the shape indicated a bottle of wine, it wasn't quite large enough to hold one. Unless it was a really short bottle of wine.

Nick rubbed his hands together, leaning toward her in anticipation. "I can't wait to see if you like it."

Her heartbeat picked up in response to his nearness. She yanked the bow off, taking her frustration out on the inanimate object in order to control her emotions and distract herself from the sexual pull he exerted over her.

Well, she was right, it was a bottle. Actually, quite a large bottle. Still, it wasn't wine, although she wished it were. No, it was perfume. And not just any perfume, either.

"It's called Ask Me Anything," Nick said, pointing to the name on the label. "I hope you like it."

She was speechless. And panic-stricken. Of course she liked it—she'd sprayed his whole bedroom with it, for heaven's sake! "Uh, I love it," she said, her voice sounding limp to her ears. "How did you know?"

As soon as the words were out of her mouth, she realized there was only one way he could've known.

She was caught!

Chapter Eight

He must've figured out what she'd done. That was why he'd bought this specific perfume and given it to her. For that matter, the reason for such a huge bottle was obvious. Because he figured she'd practically emptied her own bottle at his house!

In one of those moments of crystal clarity that happen so rarely in life, she knew precisely what she was going to do.

Die. There was no way to explain why she had taken advantage of his absence to douse his pillows with perfume.

She waited expectantly, clearing the way for God to do away with her, but nothing happened. She just kept on breathing against her will, damn it! Was a simple heart attack too much to ask given the severity of the circumstances?

Finally, Amy concluded that some things really weren't fair. Under normal circumstances, when she'd managed to do something stupid, she couldn't even faint her way out of it, so it was no wonder a heart attack was beyond her capabilities. Clearly, God was going to make her face this.

Nick managed to wrestle the bottle from her white-knuckled grip on the second try. Probably to keep her from snapping it into shards…which she could later use to slit her wrists!

"I didn't know," he said. "I just guessed." He pulled off the gold-toned cap and using the atomizer, sprayed some into the air, as though he were one of those perfume girls who waited for the arrival of unsuspecting customers in the pricey department stores.

But Amy wasn't paying attention. She was too busy gathering her wits from where they'd been scattered into the mist. His answer assuring her his purchase was merely a fluke went a long way in relieving her anxiety. It didn't do anything for the hyperventilation or the dizziness, but in a few minutes her panicked reaction would subside and she could breathe normally again.

Becoming aware of him waiting for her to comment, she smiled at the earnestness on his face. "Well, thank you, it was very thoughtful," she said, rising to her feet, fumbling with the perfume. "I don't know what to say, Nick."

"Thoughtful? I'm not thoughtful, Amy, I'm grateful! You did my laundry, after all. I hate to do laundry." He gave a mock shudder to emphasize the point. "So of course you don't have to say anything. That's the point. I am saying something, and that something is *thank you*."

She nodded absently in response to his earnest appeal, trying to pull herself together. She needed a few minutes to get herself completely under control.

"You don't like it, do you?"

His crestfallen expression grounded her enough to at least act appropriately. He'd clearly gone to a great deal of trouble, and here she was acting all weird about it. She at least owed him for that. "Are you kidding? I love it!" she exclaimed, throwing herself into his arms to prove it.

Nick laughed as he braced himself for the impact, and after a few seconds she said, "I'm going to put it in my bedroom. Why don't you turn on the television? I'll be right back."

She left the room before he could utter another word, stopping only when her bedroom door was shut securely behind her. With the bottle clutched to her chest, she made her way unsteadily to the dresser standing opposite her bed. Her appearance in the mirror startled her and she knew it was a good thing she'd left. Nerves of steel she didn't have and sooner or later, he was going to notice she was behaving strangely.

In fact, she realized now she'd wildly overreacted. So what if he had figured out her plan? Yeah, it was a bit bizarre to go spraying perfume on someone's pillow, but she couldn't be the only person who'd ever done so. Could she? And would it have been so awful to have her feelings for him finally out in the open?

Yes, she decided. The open wasn't where she was ready to be. Not just yet. She was only just now getting the hang of being a little bit daring. Downright brazen was beyond her. But she was making progress.

Setting the bottle down gently on the decorative tray that contained her small collection of perfumes, she marveled at the size of the bottle, chuckling softly as she thought about how long it would take her to empty it. She'd have more gray hair than Ted by then.

Plainly stated, the bottle was huge. In fact, compared to the other bottle of Ask Me Anything, it was gigantic. The pair looked like David and Goliath. The humorous thought comforted her and she felt more like her old self.

Which was a mix of good and bad.

She flopped backwards onto the bed, throwing her arms wide as she did. How could her simple little plan have gotten so messed up? The idea was for him to seduce her, at least subconsciously, not buy her presents!

She went over the whole thing in her mind, replaying her reasons and her goals, and despite the turnout, she still thought it had merit. Maybe everything wasn't so lost as it appeared. The ploy did make him think about her, even if not in the way she was counting on. That didn't make it a total failure.

No, in fact, maybe this was just the first step. If she came up with one plan, she could come up with another.

Feeling better she sat up, rubbing her forehead in concentration. Maybe the problem was that her first attempt was too subtle. She didn't know many men who could take a hint and Nick probably wasn't any exception.

She needed an idea that would put him physically in her presence at the time it was enacted. Something a little more dramatic and daring on her part.

However, try as she might, she couldn't come up with anything. And the harder she tried, the worse her ideas got.

A loud grumble convinced her to give it up for now. Most likely the reason she couldn't come up with anything was because she couldn't think above the noise of her stomach demanding food.

Heaving herself off the bed, she went to join Nick. They might as well eat dinner together. There were worse things she could think of than eating dinner with a gorgeous man.

Scuffing down the hallway and back into the living room, Amy was standing next to Nick before she realized she was still wearing her Scooby-Doos. As usual, she'd passed up an opportunity to make headway in her quest for his attention. It was no wonder he never thought of her as girlfriend material. Who could blame him? She never did anything to let him know she was.

Her stomach rumbled again, interrupting what was promising to be an impressive pity party. Setting her mind to her circumstances, she determined to enjoy the fact that he was here with her at this moment. "I was getting ready to have dinner. Did you eat yet?"

He rubbed his belly in reply. "No, and I'm starving. What do you have?" He checked his watch. "I can't believe I didn't think to grab something on the way over here."

Suddenly, he paused in his exuberance, shifting his feet slightly. "Look, I'm really sorry I just barged in." He looked her up and down as though he was just noticing what she wore before continuing. "It was rude, especially since it's pretty obvious you weren't expecting company. I think it'd be best if I left."

Amy grabbed his arm, pulling him around to face him. "Nick, you are not company. If you want, I'll change into some jeans and a T-shirt."

He stroked his chin, acting as though giving the matter serious thought. "No," he said, making his deliberation. "I think I can handle a woman in flannel without too much effort."

"Okay, good, cuz I'm pretty comfortable. Now, I have chili on the stove, and I'm getting ready to make some corn muffins to go with it, just as soon as I open the boxed mix. I've got plenty, if you'd like to have some."

Plenty was an understatement. That was the worst part of cooking for one person, the leftovers. They made great lunches, and some, like chili, froze well, but that didn't change the reality that leftovers emphasized her lonesome status.

"If you're sure, that sounds great to me. Thanks." He followed her to the kitchen, leaned on the counter and said, "And now that we've established how welcome I am, and that I could never be a pest..."

"I didn't say anything about *never*," she interrupted automatically. Honestly, they really did act like siblings.

Familiarity was not an advantage in the romance game.

"...can I get my chili on rice?" he continued as though she hadn't said a word.

"Rice?" It wasn't an unheard of request. She was simply unaware he liked his chili that way.

"It's how my grandmother used to make it. Probably to make it last longer." The admission of childhood poverty would've made some people self-conscious. But not Nick.

Her heart melted. "Yes, you can have rice." She reached into the cupboard and pulled out an unopened box of instant rice, pleased she had it on hand.

She made the rice and the muffins, and while they waited for everything to be finished, Nick fiddled with her broken icemaker. By the time she had everything dished up and waiting, he was washing his hands.

"It wasn't broke," he told her. "You just had some ice stuck in the shoot blocking up the whole thing."

Wiping his hands on a dry towel, he sat down at the counter. He picked up his spoon and then paused. "Do you have cheese?"

Reaching into the refrigerator without a word, Amy pulled out a bag of pre-shredded cheddar cheese. He sprinkled a mountain of it onto his dinner, before sealing the bag and handing it back to her.

"Do you want some chili to go with your cheese?" she couldn't help teasing.

"No, thanks, I'm trying to quit," he retorted, and she felt like they were returning to some common ground. It was reassuring because things had been a little tense since their impromptu wrestling match. The fact that Nick didn't seem to remember at all, while she remembered every excited heartbeat, bothered her, but she wasn't about to bring it up. If he wanted to pretend it never happened, that was fine by her. For now, anyway.

She poured them each a glass of iced tea and then sat next to him. They ate quietly for a moment, but she still wasn't comfortable with the perfume situation. Besides, she could eat her dinner in silence any night. "Thanks again for the perfume, Nick, I really do appreciate it."

Her timing was off–he was sipping his drink. She'd probably make a good waitress since they always seemed to ask how the food was just as you put a bite in your mouth.

"It's not a big deal." He wiped his mouth on the paper napkin she handed him. "I'm just glad you like it."

He looked over at her and she could tell he was pleased she'd brought it up again. She worked up her courage and then continued. "What made you think to buy that fragrance?"

He continued chewing his bite of muffin, swallowing before answering. "I didn't think of it. Not really. I was at the mall, sorta shopping around for something interesting, and this woman next to me was wearing it. So I asked her what the name was and where I could get some." He shrugged to indicate that was all there was to the story.

"I see." Amy ate her chili and sipped her tea, deflated to realize her ploy hadn't had an effect on him. It was coincidence and some other woman who inspired him to purchase the very perfume she wore all the time.

She brushed corn muffin crumbs off her fingers the way she shook off this news. She might be deflated, but she was undaunted. There was still time to work her way into his arms, and dwelling on a setback wasn't going to help her cause at all.

Putting her empty bowl into the sink, she wiped her hands on a towel and turned to face Nick, flirtation on her mind.

Only to be interrupted by his conversational foray. "Hey,

can I ask you something?"

"Sure," she said with a big grin. "Ask me anything."

"Very funny." He looked like he was about to say something more.

"What?" Amy encouraged him to continue.

"Nothing," he said. "But I did have a question."

She waited, wondering what the big deal was.

"How come women get free stuff when they shop?" He looked at her in all seriousness.

She stuttered to a halt in her thinking. She'd imagined him inquiring about something important. "What?" She tried to figure out what he was talking about, but she was clueless.

Nick stood to take his dishes to the sink, brushing by her as he did so. "When I was buying that perfume, the lady at the counter kept giving me all this free stuff to go with it. Why do they do that?"

"To convince you to buy more than you actually need." Surely he knew this?

He paused, thinking for a second, and then slowly nodded his head. "That's what I figured. Does that happen everywhere you shop?"

"No," Amy said. "Mostly at the department stores." As soon as she finished the sentence, she realized what he was getting at. She laughed. "Did you come away with some 'free' gifts?"

His sheepish glance preceded his admission. "Yeah, I got a lot of free gifts." He reached into his pocket, pulling out his keys. "Here's one of them."

She took the keys from him, her attention caught by what looked like a Swiss army knife. Opening it, she realized it was a manicure set. "Why would you need one of these?"

He pursed his lips and tilted his head to the side. "I just thought it was sorta cool. No big deal."

She handed the keys back to him and he put them in his pocket. "What else did you get?"

A full-fledged shrug accompanied his response. "An umbrella, some soap... a couple other things."

"Oh." She snapped her fingers. "That reminds me. I got you something, too."

Making her way to a nearby closet, she pulled out her offering. "You need a mop." She passed it to him. As soon as he took it, she reached back into the dark closet. "And an iron."

"Is that the closet you mentioned earlier? The one where my Christmas presents are tucked away? Cuz if it is, I want my perfume back."

He looked ridiculous holding a mop in one hand and an iron in the other, and she couldn't help but laugh. "Nick, you didn't even have the basic household supplies. How do you keep things tidy?"

"How do you know?" he asked. "Did you go snooping around while you were there?"

"No, I didn't," she said, glad she was telling the truth. "But you read my note didn't you? I had to look for a mop to clean up the mess. And I contemplated ironing your clothes. Only for a second, before I came to my senses. But in that split second, I tried to find an iron, to no avail."

"Maybe I'm just a tidy person. Maybe I don't make many messes." He pointed the mop in her direction for emphasis.

"Yeah, but still," she said, unwilling to pass up the opportunity to harass him just a little. She knew without a doubt he'd extend her the same courtesy. "You still have to occasionally mop and iron. There's no way around it." She spoke with the voice of authority.

"I do mop," he asserted. "In fact, the last time I mopped, I was scrubbing so hard the mop handle snapped in two. They don't make them very sturdy, do they?"

Amy refrained from pointing out that in all the years she'd been mopping, the handles never broke. The sponges wore out like crazy, or got so grungy you couldn't use them any more, but the handles didn't break. Maybe it was a guy thing. "What about ironing?"

"Okay, you got me there. I don't know how to iron." He waved the small appliance around, looking as if he were offering up a flag of surrender.

She was aghast. "You're kidding! How did you get to be thirty years old and not learn to iron?"

"Just lucky?"

Amy took the iron out of his hand. "Come on," she said, turning and leading the way.

"Where are we going?" Nick asked, leaning the mop against the wall before following her.

"To fill in the gaps of your education."

They reached Amy's compact but functional laundry room where she had a portable ironing board set up. Placing the appliance on the board and plugging it in to heat it up, she quickly scanned the few items of clothing hanging on a short rack waiting to be pressed. She selected a blouse that was wrinkled, but one she also knew wasn't that difficult to iron out.

"Okay, but be gentle," he urged. "It's my first time."

She rolled her eyes. She wasn't in the mood to flirt, although it amazed her to admit it. For once, she knew how to do something he didn't, and this was her chance to show him up.

"Here." She handed him the shirt. "Spread it on the ironing

board."

He twisted the shirt this way and that, but was unable to get it to lie flat. Oh, boy, Amy thought. He wasn't kidding. He really didn't know anything about this.

"Okay," she said, taking pity on him. "You watch me the first time around."

She took the shirt from him, their fingers brushing against one another slightly, and in seconds she had the garment spread perfectly and ready to go.

Picking up the iron, she held it out to him.

"What am I suppose to do with this?" he asked before taking it.

"I'm going to tell you." Lifting the collar of the shirt, she pulled out a flap of material sewn in. "The first thing you should do is check the label to see what the piece of clothing you want to iron is made of."

She let the shirt settle back into place without bothering to follow her own instructions. "Then, you set the iron temperature according to the information on the label. The iron has different heat settings, as you can see right here." She pointed to the colorful list of choices on the top of the iron.

As soon as he nodded that he understood, she spun the dial to the proper setting. "Now, once the temperature's set—"

"Wait," he interrupted her. "You didn't check to see what the shirt's made of."

She started to explain that was because she'd ironed this particular shirt a hundred times and she knew the setting by heart, but just as she opened her mouth, it occurred to her he wasn't truly pointing out her mistake. He was asking her to show him where to read the instructions from the label.

She picked up the shirt and went to him, pulling the label

out and holding it where he could see it. He bent to accommodate her shorter height, although he was careful not to actually touch her.

Not that she noticed. Much. "Right here," she said. "It says what the shirt's made of. And if you flip the tag over, it gives you instructions on precisely what setting to use on the iron."

He took the garment from her, looking at both sides of the label. "Did you know it gives you directions on how to wash and dry it too?" He looked down at her with a sideways glance.

Amy smiled. "Yes, I know. Didn't you ever notice that before?"

The slight shake of his head admitted his ignorance. "I usually cut the tag out as soon as I get the shirt home. I don't like it rubbing the back of my neck." He handed the shirt back to her. "I didn't know there were instructions for washing and ironing. I thought you just tossed them into the machine, dried them, and then hung them up in the closet. I do know not to use metal hangers." He said it as though it were an accomplishment.

Was he uncomfortable having her teach him something? Or was he just uncomfortable being around her period?

"Well, you can just hang them up," she admitted slowly. "In fact, some clothes need no ironing at all. And even the ones that do, it's not required that you iron them. They just look better if you do."

"But don't they just get wrinkled again as you're wearing them?"

She bit her lip. He had a point, one she'd often wondered about herself. "Yes, that's true, but I don't think they look as bad if they start out ironed."

It made sense to her, anyway.

Nick nodded absently, apparently trying to figure out if that was a reasonable statement. She quickly turned to lay the shirt flat on the board again. "Anyway, to continue, once the iron is turned on, you have to wait for it to heat up to the proper temperature."

"Why?"

"Why what?"

"Why do you have to wait for it to heat up to the proper temperature?" The tilt of his head indicated he was either fascinated by the lesson, or screwing with her. She would bet money she knew which one.

She gritted her teeth. All she was trying to do was show him the very basics in wardrobe care, not explain the science of the matter. She should've told him to read the manual.

Actually, now that she thought about it, was there a manual? Had anyone ever learned to iron from reading the manual? It didn't seem likely.

Nick cleared his throat. "Amy?"

She dragged her attention back to the business at hand. "You have to wait because it's easier to smooth out the wrinkles if the iron is at the right level of heat..." She trailed off. That sounded stupid even to her, and she knew what she was doing.

She tried again, with a good dose of sarcasm thrown in because she was tired. "It's a well-guarded secret, but if you keep it to yourself, I'll let you in on it." She leaned toward him and dropped her voice to a stage whisper. "If you don't wait for it to heat up, you'll be wasting your time. Different fabrics require different temperatures. It's all very scientific and a panel of geniuses figured it out a long time ago, compiling it into a very large, very dusty textbook. I can show it to you if you want."

He folded his arms across his chest and scowled. "Cute." His tone showed he didn't think so. "You don't have to get touchy about it. I only asked a simple question."

She sighed. He was right. "I'm sorry. It's just, this isn't hard, Nick. You don't need to understand why you do it a certain way. Just do it, okay?"

He shrugged one shoulder. "Fine." Putting his hand out, palm up, he said, "Proceed."

She nodded. "Thank you. Now, as I was saying, once it's been on for a little while, it'll be the correct temperature and you can begin."

"How do you know it's the right temperature?" He cringed as Amy whipped around.

"*Argh*. I thought we were just going to iron here," she said behind gritted teeth. "You just take it for granted!"

He put his hands up in front of him in surrender. "All right, all right. I forgot. Calm down."

"I am calm," she said, in a voice that showed she was lying through her still gritted teeth. "Listen, I promise you. There isn't a test after this, okay? Just *watch* and *listen*. That's all you have to do for now. Honest."

She didn't wait for his acquiescence before she went on. "Now, it is definitely hot enough to begin because we've spent about five minutes discussing whether it's hot enough to begin.

Picking up the iron, she started at the hem and moved the iron back and forth, the wrinkles disappearing magically. Nick moved closer so he could see, his brow wrinkled in concentration. She worked her way up the blouse in a smooth rhythm developed from years of practice.

Putting the iron down, she moved the shirt to the next wrinkly section, anticipating Nick's question, but it never materialized. "So," she said, finishing up the straightforward part of the project. "We've made it to the point where we have to do the arms, which are slightly more difficult, but only because they require a little more attention to detail. What we just did was fairly mindless, once you get the hang of it."

He nodded, clearly not fascinated with her speech, but determined to get through it anyway.

She stretched one of the sleeves out flat and made quick work of getting it completed, explaining bits of technique as she went.

Soon the entire garment was done and she put it on a hanger, showing Nick the end results as she did. Once it was hung on the rack, ready to be placed in her closet and worn, she faced him. "Well, what do you think?"

He ran his fingers through his hair, making her wish she could do that without freaking him out. She held back a sigh. It was weird, the way her status went from friend helping friend, to predatory female in the blink of an eye.

"It doesn't seem hard to me."

Well, hallelujah! "It's not hard," she agreed. "It's just something to be done, like laundry or dishes, that's all."

Turning, she took another shirt from the assortment waiting to be ironed. She handed it to him. "Okay, your turn."

When he stood there, staring at her blankly, she waved the shirt insistently in his direction. "Take it. Let's see what you've learned."

Tentatively, as though the fabric could possibly be alive, he took the shirt.

"Now," she directed. "What's the first thing to do?"

"Check the tag," he said, doing just that. Once he confirmed what it was made of, he set the clothing down on the ironing board and picked up the iron. He adjusted the setting accordingly. While he waited for the temperature to change, he got into position in front of the ironing board.

Amy folded her arms as he fumbled with her shirt, trying to keep from helping him. She couldn't help the smile that crossed her face, though, as she watched him trying to get everything just-so.

Once he was happy with the results, he looked at her and winked. Her heart flopped over in her chest and in that instant, trying to keep from helping him wasn't her problem. It was keeping from tackling him that occupied her mind now.

Shaking her head slightly, she refocused her attention onto his actions, not surprised to see he was actually ironing wrinkles into the fabric. "Whoa there, cowboy," she said, grabbing his arm to stop him. "You're going to make this shirt impossible to wear if you don't pay better attention to the details."

"Why?"

"This." She pointed to the deeply imbedded creases he'd created. "You can't iron the clothes if there's the tiniest little fold, otherwise you'll create more wrinkles than you do away with."

"So, now you're changing your story. You're saying this isn't as easy as it looks?"

"I'm not sure," she said. "I never thought it was hard, but maybe I'm just gifted in this area."

Proving it, she stretched the material out flat. "There, see how smooth this is? There's nothing to create a problem, right?"

He nodded in agreement and she stepped behind him, directing him with her hands on his hips to face the board. "Now," she said, wrapping her arms around him and using his hand to pick up the iron.

It was a stretch, but if she leaned her whole body into him and stood on her toes, she could see around his right shoulder. "You take the iron and you gently glide it over the material. Start at the bottom and work your way up, stroking it almost, as you work to get the job done."

The two of them worked quietly for a few seconds, neither of them paying much attention to the chore, and it wasn't long before she noticed Nick wasn't helping.

"Jesus," he said under his breath. He was standing perfectly still, his head tilted to the side, her breath fanning his neck.

She jumped back before she realized what she was doing, and now it was too late to insinuate herself back into the position of pressing herself totally into him, making him aware of every physical aspect of her body.

Flustered by what could have been, and a little embarrassed by the situation, she tried to grab the iron out of his hand, but he didn't let go like she thought he would. "*Yeow*," she yelped, shaking her hand where she'd been burnt.

"Are you hurt?" He stood the iron on the board and grabbed her hand.

He inspected her injured fingers. "It doesn't hurt that bad. Just a tiny little burn. I've been burned before."

Ignoring her comment, he held her hand up to the light, a small frown creasing his forehead. He puckered his lips slightly and she gulped, and then tensed as she felt his breath blowing gently across the palm of her hand and over the wounded area.

"What are you doing?" she asked in a small whisper.

He looked into her eyes, his face mere inches away, but he didn't say a word.

Amy was again faced with a chance to make her dream come true, and she girded herself to respond as her heart demanded. She was going to kiss him.

No, wait a minute. It looked like he was going to kiss her! That was even better.

Nick ducked his head toward her, and Amy closed her eyes to wait. With her heart pounding in her chest and the blood roaring in her ears, she tensed, afraid to move or even breathe, in case she scared him off.

His hair tickled her nose and she sighed, anticipation causing her to stand to her full height, not wanting to make him travel any further than he had to in order to answer this prayer. Her senses tingled and the excitement built to a fever pitch. Even her burnt fingertips felt the kiss.

Her eyes flew open in disbelief, not sure where she'd gone wrong.

Somehow, Nick had gotten lost on his way to their first real kiss, bypassing her lips and instead placing both her injured appendages into his mouth, gently swirling his tongue around them.

"What are you doing?" she asked again, this time in a voice considerably louder than a whisper.

He popped her fingers out of his mouth and looked them over. "I'm taking care of you," he said, his voice a rasp of noise. "First you blow on a burn, then wet it. And finally, you," he bent his head and placed his lips on both injuries. "Kiss it," he finished his remedy. "There, all better."

Not even close, Amy thought, hiding her shaking hands behind her back. "Uh, thanks," she said, hoping he wouldn't notice her heavy breathing. Honestly, she sounded as though she'd run a race.

Nick put an end to the torture, stepping back away from her. "Do you want me to finish up the shirt? Or do you want to wrestle me for it? Keep in mind, I know you cheat."

The gleam in his eye had Amy thinking maybe he wasn't so immune to her charms as he pretended, but that gleam was soon replaced by his playful chucking of her chin.

Great. She felt about twelve. "I'll finish it," she said, incapable of keeping the pout out of her voice. "You should probably get going, before it gets too late. As you can see," she pointed to her jammies. "I'm planning on an early night."

He nodded slowly, but said nothing, staring at her so intently she was afraid to swallow in case he interpreted it as…what? Anticipation? Cowardice? Stupidity?

She was too overwrought to define her actions right now. Tomorrow, over a strong cup of coffee and a bagel, she'd regroup, but tonight she was going to get into bed and pretend none of this had happened.

If she was lucky, she might believe it.

Chapter Nine

Nick buckled his seatbelt in a daze, still not sure what the hell was going on. Starting his car and heading for home, he replayed the evening.

First, he'd brought her a present. No big deal. They ate dinner, still nothing out of the ordinary. He'd even managed to keep from mentioning how cute she looked in her pajamas or commenting on their wrestling match. He was getting good at suppressing that memory. When he was awake, anyway.

Then, somehow, Amy was giving him an impromptu lesson on ironing, in a little room barely big enough to turn around in, and before he knew what was going on, all he could think about was how he'd like to stretch her out on the board as she was explaining the process.

Not that it would support their weights, but facts didn't play into his fantasies.

Shocked at the direction his brain was taking, he'd asked her some remedial questions about ironing, hoping to end the torture. But she just kept on with the instructions.

Then she suggested he take a turn, to show her what he'd learned. Deciding it would be quicker to just do as she asked and get out of there as quickly as possible, he stepped up to the plate.

Big mistake. Huge.

Handling the soft fabric of her clothes had been one thing,

but concentrating on the size and shape of the shirt had somehow filled his mind with visions of her body. The ironing exercise was a little more intimate than he was used to being with his friends.

Certain that was the worst of it, he was shocked to learn he was wrong.

As soon as he began running the hot iron over her freshly laundered shirt, her fragrance rose up into his consciousness, tantalizing and teasing. The more he moved the iron over the clothing, the stronger the scent became. Back and forth, he stroked the material, until she'd put a stop to it by pointing out that he was ruining the article.

Stunned at what he'd done, he could only stand there while she attempted to fix the problem. A few minutes and a lot of concentrating later, he was just starting to pull himself together, when she'd stepped behind him to guide his hand through the process.

Every prayer he knew ran through his mind. He was almost positive he'd even said "Jesus."

It was no use.

Even now, his back could feel the imprint of her body all the way from his shoulder blades to his waist, and he didn't like it.

Which was a blatant lie. He liked it way too much. And wasn't that the real problem?

He slammed his fist to the steering wheel in frustration, accidentally blowing the horn and garnering the attention of his fellow drivers on the road.

This could not be happening. He could not be getting hot for Amy. Could not be reliving the way her breasts felt flattened into his back.

Amy. Whom he'd known since before she even *had* breasts, for God's sake!

Okay, fine. Maybe he was starting to...feel that way. It wasn't impossible. She was attractive, fun. Why wouldn't he think about her that way?

But that didn't mean he had to continue. In fact, he wouldn't. He'd put a stop to it right now. This instant.

From now on, he'd make sure to never be alone with her. He wouldn't allow himself to think about that wrestling match that drove him crazy, or the feel of her pressed tightly up against him.

And he especially wouldn't think about how all he had wanted to do was turn around so she was squeezed up against his front instead. With very little effort, he could have wrapped himself around her, pulled her up onto her toes where he could reach her with his lips, and...

And that was another thing he wouldn't think about. The fact that in order to keep from planting one on her, he'd taken her fingers into his mouth and sucked on them instead.

No, he wouldn't think of that at all. Or at least, not much. It was simply a case of mind over matter, that was all.

Although judging from his current state of awareness, he knew it wasn't his mind that mattered.

Damn! He had to learn some better prayers, because the ones he knew weren't enough protection against what he was fighting.

* * *

Amy stifled a yawn as she turned the car off. Unbuckling the seatbelt for comfort, she settled in to wait.

And think. About last night, when Nick delivered the perfume, stayed for dinner, and helped her iron a couple of shirts. Help being a relative term.

Just reliving it raised her blood pressure. She should know, she'd spent a sleepless night going over it, again and again. Only this time, instead of focusing solely on her missteps, she made an effort to concentrate on what had gone right, and how she could use it to her advantage.

Through a lot of soul-searching honesty, she realized that she might not be an expert on men, but she would lay down good money that she'd made major progress last night. There was no way Nick was unaffected. She was thrilled. If only she'd realized it then, when she could've capitalized on it.

And she realized that as responsive as Nick was becoming, she was beating him by an easy mile. Hot didn't begin to express her need, and getting him into bed was becoming more than a project now, it was a physical necessity. Which was why she was upping the ante. The two of them needed more than opportunity, they needed bodily contact.

All of this should've been obvious to her, of course, but in all her planning and machinations, she was convinced that it would occur naturally. Like the wrestling, which was a bonus. She'd dropped the ball, however, when she failed to capitalize on it and move the game further down the field.

So, hours after Nick left last night, and dozens of discarded plans later, Amy finally hit upon her current scheme, and that was why she was sitting in her car, in the dark, on the side of a deserted stretch of two-lane highway. All that was missing was Nick coming to her rescue, and since she'd used her cell phone to call him, he should be arriving shortly. After that, she'd hop into his car and for almost an hour the two of them would be intimately alone, in the dark. The thing that made the plan work was the fact she had to drive out here anyway, after work, to check on a building project for her brother. It was an easy thing to dawdle on the site, drive around a little extra, and then allow herself to run out of gas.

She frowned when she remembered how long she'd had to drive around before the car finally sputtered and choked to a halt, but that was okay. The plan was in motion, and with any luck at all, she'd be in Nick's bed tonight.

After what had to be at least an hour later, Amy checked her rearview mirror, watching as the approaching headlights zoomed past. That was a relief. She'd already had to fend off three Good Samaritans from trying to come to her aid, assuring them over and over that someone was coming for her and she needed to wait. Although she appreciated their concern and effort, the truth was, she wasn't scared to be stuck at all. If she hadn't engineered this little disaster, that would be a different story, of course.

It was too dark to check the time on her watch, and she didn't dare turn on her inside lights, not wanting to add a dead battery to her car woes. Running out of gas was bad enough.

She smiled, amazed at how well her plan was going so far. The two-lane highway that connected the east coast of Florida to the west coast was mostly deserted, so it was the perfect place to be in distress.

She frowned. Maybe she wasn't as unconcerned as she imagined if she had to keep reminding herself she wasn't afraid?

Reaching over the console she felt along the passenger seat, making certain the brass candlestick was still where she'd put it. She wasn't sure how much protection it would offer, but it made her feel better than coming out here completely unarmed.

Sitting up straight, she watched as headlights approached from the opposite direction, hoping that this car would be Nick.

Anticipation made it seem like forever since she'd called him. When that car passed by she let out a frustrated sigh. What was taking him so long?

Another car's lights appeared and she tapped her fingers on the steering wheel, afraid to get her hopes up. As it got closer the high beams blinded her, but she didn't dare flash her lights back. She didn't want to bring any unwanted and potentially dangerous attention to herself.

The car slowed as it passed her, its brake lights glowing red in the night. Watching from her side view mirror, she tensed as the car reversed. It wasn't until the car was even with hers that she relaxed, recognizing Nick's sedan. He backed up further and then pulled off the side of the road, finally parking in front of her.

Frozen in place with the reality that her plans were about to come to fruition, Nick was out of his car and standing next to her before she even thought to open her door. He ducked his head to peer inside just as she pulled the handle and pushed. He stepped back, just avoiding getting whacked by the door. Her overhead light went on as she got out of the car, illuminating both of them. She smiled up at him.

"What are you doing all the way out here?" he all but bellowed at her. "Don't you know you could get killed sitting here in the dark, alone and helpless?"

She shut the door. She hadn't counted on him being angry. When she called him on her cell phone, his voice had shown real concern, but somewhere between talking and driving out here he'd worked himself into a towering rage.

Jumping back into his face wasn't conducive to her seduction. She didn't want him on his guard against her, and he would definitely expect her to defend herself.

Instead, she threw herself into his arms. "Oh, Nick," she said, her hands clasped tightly around his back and her face pressed against his chest. "You don't know what it's been like, sitting out here, waiting for you to arrive. I had no idea the middle of the state was so isolated, so scary. And people kept stopping and asking me if I needed help, but I kept insisting that you would be here, you wouldn't let me down."

By now she had herself convinced of her own fear and the shaking that overtook her was more real than playacting. He rubbed his hands slowly up and down her back, making soothing noises and promising it would all be okay. If she could stay here forever it would all be worth it.

A mosquito buzzed her ear and she swatted it, breaking the mood. Damn, why didn't she bring mosquito repellent? And why were the mosquitoes still around this time of year?

Nick leaned back, but he didn't let go of her. "I'm sorry I yelled at you. It's just…you scared the crap out of me! All I could think about as I was driving out here was that some murderer was going to get here first. I tried to call, but you had your cell phone turned off. Why didn't you leave it on?"

She bit her lip. She'd turned it off after calling him precisely so he wouldn't be able to call her back, but she couldn't admit that to him. "I guess I didn't realize it was off. I hardly ever use my phone, you know that. I'm sorry you were scared." She grinned in the darkness. Everything was going as planned.

"Why didn't you call your roadside assistance service? Or the police or something?" he asked as he worked his hands over her arms.

Well, rats. She hadn't thought of that one. And she couldn't think of a reasonable answer right now, not with his hands all over her. "I don't know. I guess I just panicked and called you instead. That was pretty stupid, huh?"

"No, not stupid. I'm just glad I was available. But how could you possibly have run out of gas? It just doesn't make sense. And why are you out here in the first place?"

What was this? A game of twenty questions? If she didn't do something her plans were going to come crashing into his logic, and they'd shatter into shards of absurdity. "I had to check on a building project for Ted after work. I just drove out here and didn't think about anything else."

The little white lie hung between them. She was surprised it didn't glow in contrast to the black night.

"It didn't occur to you to fill up your tank before you left town?" His skepticism all but accused her outright.

"Maybe I didn't know there weren't any gas stations out here. Look, mistakes get made, okay? And I'm fine, nothing happened." She turned away from him, guilty over her fibbing.

Lies, Amy. Big ones. Call them what they are.

He took hold of her hand and turned her back. "It's okay. I'm just freaked out by the thought of you stranded out here alone like this. I'll get over it, I promise."

She let him hold her hand as long as he wanted, which turned out to be about two seconds. Probably just as well, she thought, as she swatted another mosquito. Why couldn't she live someplace where mosquitoes died off by this time of year? "Okay, are you going to drive me home or what?"

"Drive you? No, I'm not going to drive you. I stopped by the gas station and picked up some gas."

He did what? "G-gas?" He was not following the plan. "Oh, yeah, good," she said, trying to sound convincing. How was she going to be alone in his car with him, if she was alone in her car instead? "I guess I didn't think of that. Good thing you did." Yeah, right.

She followed him over to his car where he opened his trunk. The small light inside showed a space that held nothing but a large gas can. She rolled her eyes. Too bad she didn't think to get a flat tire instead.

Traipsing behind him as he headed to the back of her car, she stumbled into his back. Nick fell forward slightly, the gas can sloshing as he tried to right himself.

"Sorry," she said. "I tripped."

"No problem." He stepped away from her as though burned. "Which side of your car do you fill up on?"

"The driver's side," she said, a pout entering her voice. Why was he putting gas in her car instead of comforting her some more so she could make a move on him?

"There," Nick said when he was done fueling her vehicle. The air smelled like gasoline and it only emphasized the completely unromantic atmosphere. She was running out of time to do something.

The problem was, this part of the plan hadn't been thought out. She honestly believed that he would take over as soon as he arrived and all she'd have to do was gently guide him.

He took over, all right, just not the way she wanted. In fact, if she waited for him to make the first move she was going to die a virgin.

Nick left her side and she watched him shut the trunk of his car, her eyes adjusted to the night, wishing she'd taken the opportunity to fake a twisted ankle when she tripped into him. Honestly, she was learning some things about herself that were hard to overcome. Not only was she too subtle, she wasn't sneaky either. How would she ever get him to notice her if she couldn't find a single truly devious skill she could count on?

As he made his way back to her car she couldn't ignore the warmth that flowed through her veins or the way her heartbeat picked up. After he tucked her into the front seat, she started the car and rolled down her window. He leaned his forearms on the frame watching her. The glow from her instrument panel lit up the inside of her car enough that she could make out his expression.

He was frowning. Oh for pity's sake, she thought. What now? "Why are you looking at me like that?"

"I'm wondering why you have a candlestick on the seat next to you."

"*Er*, candlestick?" Her voice faded and fortunately it was too dark for him to see what she knew was her red face or the evasive way she avoided his eyes, even though she was sure he couldn't read anything in them.

"Yeah," he said. "A candlestick, right there." He pointed and Amy turned her head to look.

Hmm, maybe she could tell the truth on this one? "Oh, I brought it with me just in case my car broke down in the middle of nowhere. I'm not totally stupid, y'know."

She waited for him to say something, but he let the opportunity to comment on her brains pass him by. "Good, I'm glad you thought that far ahead," he said, although he sounded skeptical that a candlestick was much of a weapon. "Now," he stood up and hit the roof with his palm, "I'll follow you back into town and then I've got to get home and go to bed. I'm whipped. I didn't sleep well last night."

Amy felt torn by guilt at dragging him out on a wild goose chase in the dark, then her ears perked up at what he said. He didn't sleep well either?

Oh, yes, that was good to hear, and desire oozed its way

through her system. He wasn't waiting for her to respond to his admission, which was good, because the only thing running through her mind was to ask if he wanted some company in his bed.

And while that wouldn't be subtle or sneaky, she wasn't quite brave enough to say the words. With a defeated little sigh, she waited while he got into his car and pulled out onto the road behind her before she led the way back to city lights and more lonely nights.

* * *

Amy paced her living room while she waited and fretted over how long crab dip could sit out and still be safe to eat. Nick was supposed to be here any minute and she was more than a little nervous. The daring scope of this plan took her breath away.

It had taken her a few days to come up with this scheme after her last fiasco. Days of wracking her brain while still maintaining a normal demeanor, doing her job, and interacting with the people who knew her best.

Acknowledging the reality she'd gotten nowhere with smelling up his pillows with perfume or stranding herself in the boonies, she finally hit upon the idea to rework the old adage that said "the way to a man's heart is through his stomach" into "the way to Nick's heart is through football." So, she invited him over to watch the game, but her real motive was to get him drunk and have her way with him.

Just the possibility of the evening's agenda working made her jumpy and hot. She opened the cooler by the couch and grabbed an ice-cold beer. Popping the top she took a swig then put the freezing can against her forehead and rolled it back and forth, but it didn't cool the fire completely.

The doorbell rang and she took another sip, this one bigger than the first. Putting the can down she patted her hair into place, stalling for time and making sure she didn't go racing to the door.

She swung the door open and stood face to face with her victim...*er*, true love. No sooner did she open her mouth to speak than Nick reached out and put his finger under her chin, lifting her face up for inspection.

He stared down at her forever, or so it seemed as she waited for him to kiss her. Just like she'd done all her life.

He leaned closer and she went up on her toes. He squinted his eyes and she closed hers. "What's that red mark on your forehead?"

Amy's eyes flew open, but not faster than her mouth did. "Mark?" She was having a hard time switching gears from answered prayers to mundane observations.

"Right here." He released her chin and brushed his thumb against her forehead. "You have a red mark. I was just wondering where it came from."

Her forehead? It must be from the beer can. "Oh, I must've bumped it or something." Why was he always going off track? Couldn't he just once imagine her naked or something?

Taking a deep breath, she stepped back. "You're late," she accused and redirected the conversation.

He ducked his head before looking up. "I was watching replays of the early games on the sports channel. I guess I lost track of time."

Amy rolled her eyes. Her crab dip was room temperature because he was watching reruns? Unbelievable. And the crackers were probably stale, too.

Looking on the bright side, she knew at least the beer was

cold. And since that was the important part of the plan she couldn't get too mad. The crackers and dip were just to make him thirstier anyway.

"Well, at least tell me you didn't eat anything. I've got crab dip and I'm going to make up some hotdogs later."

"Nope, didn't eat a thing." He followed her into the living room. Flopping onto the couch he said, "In fact, I'm just about starving."

"Well, good. Help yourself to the dip," she said as she sat next to him. "The beer is in the cooler." She pointed to his left then grabbed the remote and tossed it to him.

Before long the game was on and Nick was leaning forward offering advice to the coaches on the sidelines.

By Amy's count, he wasn't drinking enough beer, so she kept handing him crackers dipped in crab.

When he was on his third can, she said, "Let me know when you're ready for a hot dog. I've got tater tots, too, just for you."

"Cool. Did you get the green ketchup?" he asked hopefully.

"I still have the same bottle from the last time you were here. You do realize they make it green for kids, right?"

"That's cuz kids are adventurous. Live dangerously, Amy. Eat the green ketchup."

Little did he know, she thought as she handed him another cracker with crab dip on it. He popped it in his mouth and washed it down with a sip of beer. This was going so well she almost felt bad. Then he leaned back and stretched his arms over his head, his sweatshirt riding up to reveal the trail of dark hair that disappeared into his jeans. Amy swallowed. She didn't feel bad at all.

As Nick leaned forward and set his beer on the table, he looked up at her and rubbed his stomach. Interpreting that to mean he was still hungry, she headed to the kitchen to get the tater tots and hotdogs going.

Thirty minutes later, she returned to the living room to find him lying face down on the couch. Oh, no! Had he had too much beer? That possibility never occurred to her since Nick wasn't exactly a heavy drinker.

Setting the hotdogs-and-tots laden tray down, she smoothed back his hair, surprised to find it wet with sweat. He moaned and she dropped next to him on the very edge of the couch, genuine concern taking over her thoughts. "Nick? Are you okay?"

He opened one eye and peered at her. "No. I think I'm dying."

"What's wrong?" she wanted to know. "Is there anything I can do?"

He tried to roll over; she stood up so he could. "I think the crab dip was bad, I feel like I swallowed fire. And razor blades."

From this angle, she had to admit he did look a little green. Guilt washed over her. "What can I do? Do you need me to call an ambulance? Get a cold compress? Anything? Just tell me."

He started to rise. "I just need to go home. I'll be okay once I can get to my house."

"You can't drive like this," she insisted. "Let me get my keys. At least let me take you home, since it's my fault this happened." Oh, God, it was her fault. Her stupid, selfish fault.

She was heading to the hall to fetch her keys when he stopped her. "No, Amy, please. I really don't want you to drive me home. Really."

He joined her in the hall and opened the door. "Ah, fresh air. I feel better, really."

He was lying and they both knew it, but she kept her mouth

shut. It wasn't easy, but she did it, because she knew he wanted to leave with some dignity in tact. "Okay," she agreed. "But promise me you'll call me if you need anything? Anything at all?"

He promised. Amy watched as he pulled out of her driveway before she grabbed her keys and followed him home. It was the least she could do. The very least.

Chapter Ten

Three days later, fully recovered from his encounter with Amy's crab dip, and not holding a grudge, Nick stepped out of the shower, stubbing his toe. Deciding the damage didn't require a bandage, he toweled off. Drying his hair before dropping the towel in the clothes hamper, he brushed his teeth, thought about flossing, decided mouthwash would be good enough, then went into his bedroom. The light on his answering machine flashed insistently. Thinking it might be the front office, he hit the "play" button and waited.

"Nick!" Amy's voice came at him loud and clear. "Get over to my place as quick as you can." The message ended with a little shriek.

He immediately snatched up the phone and dialed. When there was no answer at her apartment, he didn't bother leaving a message. There was no time.

He slammed down the receiver and pulled open dresser drawers, pulling out whatever he could grab. He dressed and ran out of the room, stopping only for his keys before bolting out the door at full speed.

Heart pounding and thoughts whirling, he tried to come up with a plan for when he got there, but the only thing he could think of was to drive as fast as he could.

After a hair-raising few minutes, amid the sound of squealing tires, he pulled into the parking lot of her building. He reached to unbuckle his seat belt, but discovered he'd never fastened it. Slamming the car door hard, he didn't bother to lock it.

Racing up the steps to her apartment, he impatiently mashed the doorbell with his finger. Counting to ten, he made it to four before he pounded the doorbell again. Just as he was about to break the door down, it opened, revealing Amy, wearing a towel on her head and a nubby pink bathrobe belted at her waist.

"Oh, Nick." She pulled the door open wide, genuinely surprised to see him. "What are you doing here?"

"What am I doing here?" he asked incredulously. "Didn't you leave a panicked message on my answering machine, telling me to get here as quickly as possible?" He ran his fingers through his own damp hair. Trying to dry them off, he rubbed them on his shirt, startled when they got stuck in a hole in the side. He looked down. Wasn't this the shirt he'd used the other day to wash his car?

He pulled it out from his body. Sure enough, there were the grease marks.

"Oh, you're right, I did leave a message," Amy said, blushing. "But that was yesterday. Didn't you wait to hear the date and time?"

"Date and time?" His machine had recorded no date and time. Puzzled, he soon realized that was because he'd never reset it after the last power outage. "I guess my machine's not working right."

"Oh." She turned, holding the door for him. "Well, you see, there was this spider," she began.

Nick shut the door behind him. "Spider?" he asked. He almost got himself killed getting here because of a spider?

"Yes, you know, eight legs, walks up walls, eats flies?" She put her hand up to steady the towel on her head which kept slipping off to the left.

"Spider?" He still couldn't make himself believe it. "Not an ax murderer? Or a burglar? Or a rabid dog?" He put his hands on his hips. "A spider?"

She had the audacity to smile. "I'm sorry, Nick, but I panicked. If it makes you feel better, it was a really big spider." She held her fingers apart a good three inches to show him just how big it was.

"Why didn't you call Ted?"

"Oh, please," she said, dismissing that possibility. "Ted's a bigger wuss than I am when it comes to spiders." She leaned against the wall, shoving the towel back on her head. "Now, I could've called Janelle. But with her being pregnant again, I don't know, I just didn't want to bother her."

"But you don't mind bothering me, right?" he asked, a slight smile on his face. "You're getting kinda demanding in your old age, aren't you?"

He expected some sort of comeback, but all he got was a smile that intrigued him. "Why didn't you answer the phone when I called?" he asked, leaning his weight on one foot and putting his hands in his pockets. He couldn't believe it when the fingers of his right hand were visible under the cut-off part, poking out through the ripped pocket. *Aren't these the shorts I painted the garage in?* He lifted the shirt to have a look. Yup, they sure were. There was dried paint all over them. In fact, they were positively crusty with it.

"When did you call?" She tilted her head to the right. Probably to compensate for the towel.

"When?" he repeated. "Just a couple of minutes ago, before I raced over here like a lunatic."

"I guess I must've been in the shower," she said. "Did you leave a message?"

"No, I didn't leave a message." He tried to think, but thoughts of a soapy Amy kept getting in the way.

And that was precisely why he was supposed to be avoiding her. That and her deadly crab dip.

Tearing his mind away from the dangerous visions of a wet, slippery Amy, he finally remembered why he hadn't left a message. "I was too busy coming to your rescue."

"I'm sorry, Nick. I guess I didn't realize I sounded quite that…frightened on the phone." She patted his arm. "But thanks for coming to save me."

Nick wiggled his toes in delight. Then wiggled them in amazement. Hey, where's my socks? It was then he realized just how panicked he'd been. It was no wonder he was dressed like he was.

Finally assured that she wasn't in danger, that it had been a little thing after all, he relaxed. "So, where is this huge spider now?" he asked, making conversation because she just looked so cute with that towel threatening to bend her backwards. Why didn't she just take it off?

"I killed it," she said. "With one of Michael's shoes." She tightened the robe's belt with a proud little pull.

Well, there went his relief all to hell. "Michael's shoes?"

"*Um*, yeah," Amy said, as if the explanation for that was obvious. "I didn't want to use one of mine." She shuddered.

Nick didn't want to know why Michael's shoes were at Amy's house, or when they'd been left there. He'd been doing his best to take Janelle's advice. Amy was an adult, and he just had to deal with that. His way of dealing was to not think about it. Besides, he'd been feeling uncomfortable lately: as if they might be fooling around behind Michael's back.

He cleared his throat. "Well, if you don't need me for anything," he turned to leave.

"Oh, but I do need you." Amy grabbed his arm and pulled him down the hall. Once she made sure he was following her willingly, she let go.

He refused to watch the way her hips swayed just below the belt cinched around her tiny waist. Or how the hair that escaped from beneath her towel curled innocently down her back, beckoning him to wrap the strands around his fingers.

Actually, to his credit, he tried hard not to notice any of those things, but the harder he tried, the harder he got.

He followed her straight into the bedroom, stepping over a pile of sheets lying in the middle of the floor. Determined not to look at Amy, he looked around her bedroom instead.

Big mistake.

He started with the walls, which were painted a celery green. Around the top of the room ran a border of flowered paper in varying shades of purple and pink. A wooden cupboard contained a television, VCR, and an impressive collection of movies. A walk-in closet was off to his right, a master bathroom to his left. His gaze ran over the dark purple carpet, stopping dead when they encountered a pale pink bra sprawled carelessly on the floor. He quickly looked at the only thing in the room he hadn't perused. Her king-sized bed, which took up almost the whole of one wall. Why did she need such a big bed?

"*Ahem.*"

He brought his attention back to Amy, and fear ran through his gut when she stopped at the side of the bed and crooked her finger at him, coaxing him to join her. Well, he wanted it to be fear, but he was afraid it was really anticipation. He joined her, too weak to resist.

He stared down into her eyes, and then even further down, to where the vee of her robe gaped open, the tops of her rounded breasts clearly visible from his height advantage. He brought his eyes back to her face, shocked at what he was thinking. This was Amy, not someone you spent a little intimate time with and then left behind. The realization that this was true scared him. He couldn't just walk away. He had to run.

She ran her tongue around her lips. His throat went dry. She put her hands on her hips; he fisted his hands at his sides in order to keep from reaching for her.

And that's when he knew it. Knew it without a doubt. He was doomed.

Her raised eyebrows seemed to be asking a question. He was terrified he knew what that question was, and pathetic as he was, he already knew what his answer was going to be.

"Here, grab one of these," Amy said, taking hold of the mattress handles provided by the factory.

When he just stood there, she said, "I need you to help me flip the mattress. Since you're here anyway."

He blinked. "Sure."

Well, this wasn't quite what he was thinking, but he was glad. Almost. Turning slightly away so she wouldn't notice the effect she'd had on him in these intimate quarters, he grabbed his handle and heaved.

Nothing. He glanced at Amy, raising one brow.

"We have to do it on one, two, three, or it'll never work," she explained. "Ready?"

He nodded and she counted. On three, they heaved together. It wasn't pretty, but they managed to get the mattress upright. Checking to see if she was okay, he noticed the towel had finally fallen off. "Hold on, I can't see," she said, reaching up with one hand to brush the hair from her eyes. "Okay, now, we have to try to scoot it a little bit this way, before we let it just sorta timber down."

Doing their best to scoot the bottom toward them while still holding the top straight, they managed to move it a couple of inches. "Hmm," Amy said. "I didn't realize it would be this hard."

"Who usually helps you do this?" he asked.

"Actually, this is my first time," she admitted. "It didn't look that difficult when the delivery guys set it up, and I actually thought I could muscle it around by myself, but now, I don't know. I'm awfully glad you came by."

He knew she probably could muscle it around and get the job done, but it would take some planning on her part. Ready to be done with the job, he said, "Okay, what next?"

"Haven't you ever flipped a mattress before?"

"Why would I flip a mattress?" he wanted to know.

She shook her head, her still damp hair beginning to curl up on the ends. "Never mind," she said. "Okay, on the count of three, we just let go and it'll fall where we want it. Roughly. I hope." She grinned up at him. "One, two, three."

He jumped the gun and let go just before she said *three*. Before Amy could let go of her side, the mattress started to fall and her fingers got tangled. Letting out a little shriek, she grabbed hold of Nick's shoulder and tried to yank her hand free. Already off balance, this was all it took to topple him.

Down they both went in a tangle of elbows and knees. She on her back on the cantilevered mattress, and he facedown on top of her.

Stunned for the moment, they stared at each other, their

breath mingling in rapid pants. Nick felt her heart beating against his chest and the realization of where he was finally sank in.

He broke away first, afraid of what she would see in his eyes. Lifting slightly, he dropped his gaze, only to notice her robe had come open. He closed his eyes and said the quickest prayer he could come up with, but it was no use. His eyes had been quicker, and his brain was greedy with the image.

All his illicit imaginings about this woman paled in comparison to the reality and he was hard again in an instant.

Horrified at his reaction, he moved to stand, but she restrained him. The slight pressure of her hands on his back held him immobile.

"Don't," was all she said.

It was all the permission he needed. With a groan that came from deep inside, layered in years of neglect and denial, he rested his weight fully on her once again, and he was surprised when she lifted her hips into him. He pressed into her in response, and she adjusted to accommodate him.

Nick was lost.

No. He was home. Finally.

She clouded his senses. She was all he could see, all he could feel, all he could smell. Her breath sounded like music in his ears, coming in short little bursts. For his part, he wasn't sure he was breathing, so dizzy was he with need.

With all but one of his senses focused on Amy, it was no wonder he wanted to taste her. Leaning down slightly, he put his lips on hers. Slowly, so not to frighten her.

But she was having none of that. Wrapping her arms around his shoulders, she pulled him tightly to her, deepening the kiss and rocketing his desire up a notch.

He couldn't do this, he reminded himself from somewhere far away. This wasn't a walk-away type of encounter. He was in way over his head. It wasn't part of the plan. But all his rational thoughts flitted past him like bits of dandelion fluff, too insubstantial.

He didn't know how long they remained that way, locked together in discovery on her bed, but when he finally lifted his head it was to find his hand inside her robe, molding her soft breast to fit his hand. Somehow, he'd rolled to the side, to give her breathing room, or him better access, he wasn't sure which. Didn't care.

God, she was so perfect. And he was going to burn in hell for this. But the way he saw it, he was burning in hell right now, so he might as well have a fiery memory to sustain him.

Lowering his head to her nipple, he drew it into his mouth. She moaned and the composure he had left hanging by a thread fled. Flames shot through his gut and he knew he was never going to forget this moment in time, no matter how hard he tried.

"Well, isn't this cozy?" a snide voice intruded.

Nick jumped back in shock, trying to understand where the voice had come from.

"Michael! We were, uh," Amy's voice trailed off as she fumbled with her robe, trying to tuck it around her body, looking hopelessly for the belt. It was tangled around Nick's thigh. He pulled it loose and handed it to her, then pulled the edges of the garment together securely, covering her awkwardly but adequately. As close as he'd been to losing his mind, he was having a hard time getting grounded in harsh reality.

From what he could see, Amy didn't appear to be faring much better. Her hair was a knotted mess and her lips were obviously swollen. Her face flamed from embarrassment, but she was looking him squarely in the eye, her head held high.

"I see you don't mind giving Nick what you wouldn't give me," Michael's taunting voice continued on.

Amy stood and Nick watched her rise a good inch taller as she stiffened her spine. "You are a rude, unbelievably arrogant, conniving bastard and the only thing that surprises me more is that I didn't see it before now." She lifted her chin for emphasis and Nick almost applauded.

"Yeah, well, you're not quite what I thought you were either," Michael sneered.

"That's enough," Nick said, quiet fury infusing his tone at the way the other man talked to Amy.

Granted, the two of them had been minutes away from making love. Maybe even seconds. And her boyfriend had caught them. But that didn't give Michael grounds for insulting her. Nick would answer for this one. "I'm the one to blame," Nick said. "I took advantage of the situation. If you've got anything to say, say it to me."

He knew his tone begged Michael to say something, but he couldn't help it. For months he'd restrained his distaste for this man. How nice it would be to finally exorcise some of it.

"Oh, I don't think so, Nicky boy. Amy's not one to be taken advantage of. Believe me, I've tried. Isn't that right, Ames?"

Nick didn't understand what was going on between the two of them. Michael should be upset at *him*, not throwing cheap shots at his girlfriend. Everyone knew Amy wasn't promiscuous, so the fault had to be Nick's.

"What are you doing here, Michael? Got an overabundance of poison you need to spew on the unsuspecting?" Her grip on the robe's edges was white-knuckled and Nick realized she was more upset than she let on.

He reached out to comfort her, then pulled his hand back, uncertain of her feelings where he was concerned. He'd put her in a nightmarish situation after all.

"I came to get my shoes, the cooler we used for the beach, and," he said, waving something small before his face. "I brought back the key to your front door. I'll just leave it on the dresser. Or better yet…" He tossed it to Nick, a sneer on his face. A look that seemed far more natural than the face of pleasantness he usually wore. "Maybe you'd like to have it." He started to turn away, then stopped. "Oh, Nick, I do have something to say to you. I got a pretty good show while I was standing here. I'm not much of a voyeur, too much of a team player, you see. But, I hope it was as good for you as it was for me," he said, and then he was gone.

Nick was on his feet in an instant, ready to pulverize Michael for the things he'd said. One look at Amy's suddenly defeated appearance, though, and his need for retribution disappeared, replaced with a need to consider her feelings over his.

Nick cleared his throat, sat down, stood up, then ran his hand over the back of his neck. "Amy, it'll be all right. He's upset, and he should be. What I did was really, really wrong. Once I catch up to him and explain, he'll understand. And once I leave for the new job, the two of you can get back to normal."

He'd tried to be helpful, even considerate. He'd tried these things even though it just about killed him to offer to patch things up between the two of them. He'd rather eat a can of dog food topped with raisins, but he'd do it. For her.

"Nick," she said, her voice husky and quiet. "Do you ever think that maybe all your plans are just a way of avoiding the moment? That this way, you can always be going to somewhere, or coming from somewhere, but you never actually have to commit yourself to what's going on right this minute?" She looked up at him, tucking her hair behind her ear.

"I don't understand," he said, waiting for her to explain.

She shrugged and bent to pick up the bra that was still on the floor before heading to the bathroom. Turning in the doorway, she said, "Michael and I broke up. It was best for both of us, but it was I who finally decided I was tired of taking the leftovers of life, while I leave the main courses sitting untouched."

She paused, waiting, before finally saying, "Goodbye, Nick."

She shut the door quietly behind her.

Nick supposed he should leave, and he got up to do just that, but as he headed out of the room he couldn't shake the feeling he should've asked her, begged her if necessary, to make him understand.

* * *

Stupid, stupid, stupid!

Amy banged her head against the back of the bathroom door, trying to knock some sense into herself.

It was no use, she figured. She was never going to take charge of her life. She'd been unable to even come up with a plan to seduce Nick. Oh, she'd tried. She'd tried a lot. She considered showing up at his house in the middle of the night, but couldn't come up with a single plausible reason to do so.

She sprinkled some of her perfume on his pillow, so every time he went to bed he'd make the connection to her, but for some reason that didn't work as well as she thought it would.

She ran out of gas on a deserted stretch of road east of town somewhere and called him to come rescue her. The only thing that got her was mosquito bites and a sleepless night.

Then she practically killed him with crab dip. She still hadn't forgiven herself for that.

She pondered showing up at his office dressed in nothing but a long coat and a big red bow. This one sounded like a lot of fun, until she reminded herself that he didn't actually have an office. Even if he did, there was no way she could show up there in less than a two-piece bathing suit, which would make her look absurd instead of sexy.

No, that definitely wouldn't work.

Then fate stuck a perfect opportunity in her path. When she'd left that message on his machine, it didn't even occur to her to use the spider as a means to an end. Even when he was pounding on her door and standing in her entryway, the thought still hadn't clicked in her consciousness.

Fortunately, her subconscious must've been working overtime, because when the idea to have him help with her mattress came, she'd been astounded at her devious brilliance. She was already in the middle of changing her sheets so the plan fit right in and looked natural.

And it had almost worked. Way, way better than she ever dreamed it would, had her dreams ever been that steamy.

She hadn't intended to fall on the mattress. That had been a stroke of genius she couldn't take credit for. Her big plan was to put the idea into his head and have him act on it. Make him realize he wanted her, push him past his resistance.

The whole thing was going perfectly, until Michael interrupted so completely. It was some kind of ghastly replay of her teenage attempt when the police had caught her.

She should've been upset at his interference, but the truth was, she was far more concerned with Nick at that point.

Michael and his opinion of her was something she didn't have time to worry about.

Hot tears slipped slowly down her face as she realized that nothing was as it seemed. Or maybe it was exactly as it seemed. She didn't know anymore. At this point, the only thing she did know for certain was that Nick might have been hot for her a few minutes ago, but he didn't love her. If he did, he wouldn't let Michael get away with the things he said, and he wouldn't have let a bathroom door deter him.

It was hopeless.

She was hopeless.

And that's what it boiled down to. This whole fiasco could be placed at her doorstep. Literally. Because of her dishonesty and manipulations.

She caught a glimpse of herself in the mirror, all disheveled and confused.

How did Nick feel? Was it possible he didn't understand her intentions? Had she made the rules of the game too hard?

He might've understood on some superficial level that she was willing, but what would he understand if she just whipped off her robe and said, "Take me, I'm yours"? What would he do then?

For that matter, what would he think, how would he react, if she just gathered the courage to tell him straight to his face that she loved him? The thought sent a shiver of anticipation up her spine.

Now that would put the ball in his court. He would have to deal with her emotions. Could she risk the heartache?

She might not like how he dealt with her love, but it would be settled once and for all at least. And for her, the declaration would be an act of independence. A show of force. A true demand, not a game of Clue.

Could she do the unthinkable? Was she that brave?

What do you have to lose?

Shut up, Amy told her Daring Side. I almost have this figured out on my own, I don't need you coming in at the last second, hogging all the credit.

Well, well. What happened to little Miss Sugar? She turned herself into Miz Spice Girl?

Damn straight, Amy said with a firm nod.

With a handful of tissues, she sealed the deal.

Chapter Eleven

It had been two days since the scene in Amy's bedroom. Two days since he'd damn near done something he'd fantasized about for weeks, but had didn't have the nerve to act on.

And for those same two days he refused to leave his house. He hid out like a hunted fox with hounds baying in his ear.

Nick sipped his coffee and stared out the window, noticing the blanket of pine needles and the browning grass. They were into the dry season now and the grass would go dormant for the winter. A cold front had come through yesterday, and while it didn't drop the temperatures much, it did put a huge dent in the humidity. Maybe he'd get some raking done.

One thing was certain; he had to do something to take his mind off Amy. Going over and over the other day in his mind was putting him on the verge of combusting.

He shook his head. He was going to come busting right out of his jeans if he wasn't careful.

The ringing phone made him jump and he would've spilled his coffee if he hadn't finished it. The interruption was so welcome he almost pulled a muscle running to the phone.

"Hello?" he said, picking up the receiver before the second ring, afraid the person on the other end would hang up before he could get there.

"Nick Granger?" a gravely voice asked.

"Speaking." Setting the cup on the kitchen counter he

leaned back, wincing as the cold tile contacted his naked back.

"Hey, buddy, this is Wallace from the front office. You remember me?"

Nick rolled his eyes. He remembered him. "What can I do for you, Wallace?"

"Yeah, 'pears we got a little problem with one of the cheerleaders you're going to work with." Wallace ended with a wheezy cough.

"Problem? What kind of problem, Wally?" He needed another problem right now. Couldn't get enough problems. No, sir.

"Uh, it's Wallace, Nick, not Wally. I don't go in for that nickname shit. No offense, if you know what I mean." It wasn't a question and Nick made a mental note that Wally, *er*, Wallace was touchy about his name.

"Anyway," Wallace went on, "one of the girls hurt her back. Sprained a muscle during practice and the front office was wondering if you could move up your transfer date."

"What do they want me to do? Has she seen a specialist?" He stepped over to a bulletin board and flipped the calendar to December, noting he should've done that already. He was slipping.

"Well, I thought you were our specialist, Nick. Ain't that what we hired you for?"

He had him there. He'd made it very clear on his resume he was available for whatever position they needed to fill. "Okay, Wallace, suppose you give me a complete rundown so I get the whole picture?"

"Okay, it's like this. One of the cheerleaders hurt her back doing some kind of lickety split cheerleader maneuver."

He pinched the bridge of his nose as Wallace went on.

"Doc says she can't perform for a month or so. Problem is, she's one of our most popular girls, if not the most popular. Seems she's got some special considerations the club wants to protect."

"What kind of special considerations?" He almost didn't want to know.

"Well, her name is DeeDee. We call her Double D, if you know what I mean."

It took Nick about half a second to realize Wallace was commenting on her bra size.

"When do they want me there, and what exactly do they want me to do? Follow her onto the field and act as her living bra?" He was starting to get pissed off. It would be different if they were truly concerned about DeeDee's injury, but they were only concerned about her jiggle quotient with the fans. And he was fixing to be part of this group? God, help him.

Wallace guffawed. "Damn, that was funny. You're a real funny guy, Nick. Listen, you just get yourself on a plane and get here in the next week or so and we'll get you all settled in. DeeDee can't get out of bed until then anyway, doctor's orders."

Nick sighed. "I'll see what I can do, Wallace." He hung up the phone and slumped his shoulders. In order to get there in a week, he'd have to miss Christmas with his family. He could still make Ted's Christmas party, though the thought didn't bring him much comfort.

The job he'd wanted for as long as he could remember was just past this cheerleader gig. He could almost touch it, he was so close. But he was beginning to doubt he had the stamina to even make the effort.

Nothing was clear anymore. He didn't know what he was supposed to do. All his plans had been cluttered up by a single afternoon with Amy. A few incendiary minutes and he was a goner. Brought down by a raging hard-on.

What was he? Twelve?

This could not go on. He had to do something.

He headed to his bedroom, determined to take matters into his own hands and try to clear his thinking.

* * *

Back and forth, back and forth, again and again Nick pulled and tugged, straining his arms and breaking out in a sweat across his forehead and chest. His breathing labored, muscles screaming, he couldn't stop now. He was determined to exorcise the memory of that mind-searing mattress romp he'd shared with Amy, and short of jumping her bones, this was one of the only ways he knew of.

Unfortunately, the more he tried to forget about it, the harder it got.

Finally, out of breath and exhausted, he realized he could keep on going until the palms of his hands blistered and bled, but he would never be free of the feeling of her hot little body pressed up against his, nothing separating the two of them but a few flimsy layers of cotton. The memory of how he'd cupped his hand around her soft breast, how he'd shaped it to fit his palm, was burned into his brain, an unrelenting reminder of what he could've had if not for Michael's interruption.

Still he kept trying. Faster and faster he worked, but it was no use. He couldn't get relief from the salacious thoughts that ran wild in his head.

Shit! He was a masochistic bastard.

Thank God the rake finally snagged on a tree root, forcing him to stop. He caught his breath while he checked the tines.

Leaning the rake on a nearby tree, he wiped his face with the towel tucked into the waistband of his shorts. Looking around the yard at the proof of his tireless efforts, he counted seventeen piles of pine needles. The ground was raked to bare earth in some spots.

It was hopeless and he knew it.

He forced himself to just give up and face what he'd been running from practically all his life.

He was in head-over-heels, hot steamy sex in love with Amy. His best friend's sister. Practically his own sister, he'd been telling himself forever. But the fact was, that wasn't true, and he'd always known it.

Acknowledging that thought made him feel marginally better, but it still didn't solve the problem of what he should do.

What he wanted to do was run like hell.

But if that was true, why was he still here, in this rinky-dink town at thirty years old? He should've left years ago, if that's what he really wanted.

No, the fact was, he wanted Amy. He just didn't have the courage to risk either giving up his dreams or asking her to give up hers. He knew how much this small town and having her family close by meant to her. She wasn't going anywhere.

A circling shadow drew his attention skyward. At first, he thought it was a buzzard, which would've been a fitting symbol for the mess he'd made of his life. But as he followed the bird's lazy patterns, he realized it was a hawk. He continued to watch the relentless wheeling, letting his mind absorb and accept the reality that was his tortured condition.

The hawk's circling continued for a couple minutes, deceptively monotonous and calming. Until he swooped down at an alarming speed.

Just like that. The circling had been a ruse. A pretense. First he circled aimlessly, then swooped with a vengeance.

Changing the course of his life with a split second decision.

Nick imagined that hurtling toward the ground at increasing speed would require a certain amount of courage, no matter how many times you'd done it.

Unfortunately for him, he'd never done it. He'd never had the courage to change the course of his life with a split second decision. All of his decisions were based on plans he'd made more than ten years ago, and they'd been good plans. Great plans even. In fact, he'd liked them so much he allowed the plans to take the place of actually making choices with his life.

Why?

Because he was afraid to throw himself hurtling to ground. Afraid someone would find out he wasn't what he pretended to be. That he was not even worthy of the love and loyalty of his own parents, how could he possibly expect someone as fine and good as Amy to love him?

The hawk flew just above the tree line, a snake dangling from his talons. He had what he set out for. All it took was a compelling need.

Nick had a powerful need. He was going to throw himself into the air and let the wind have his destiny. Whether she wanted him or not, he was going to give himself this chance to be free.

Leaving the rake against the tree, he moved toward the house, kicking up a pile of pine needles and giving a loud whoop as he did.

Oh yes, Nick Granger was done with lazy, aimless circles. He was going to swoop. And baby, he was going to swoop with a vengeance.

Chapter Twelve

Nick checked his hair in the rearview mirror, patting down a piece that was sticking up. One of the disadvantages of having a sunroof.

He should've left it closed, but he wanted to feel the wind in his hair, feel it whistling past him as he drove along, confirming his resolve in an elemental way.

Flipping down the visor, he checked his teeth in the vanity mirror. A quick once over, turning his face side to side, and he was left with nothing else to inspect. He'd already changed his clothes three times before deciding he would just flip a coin. It took three tosses before he ended up with the outfit he had on.

He was worse than any coward. Nervous of meeting someone he'd known almost his whole life. Pathetic. That's what he was.

He knew it, but still he lingered.

It had taken him a little while to track Amy down. He'd tried her office all morning, but got no answer. He decided she really needed a secretary, although he'd never thought so before.

From there he phoned her apartment several times over a period of hours. He finally gave up and called Ted to see if he knew where she was. He said he didn't, and asked if Nick had thought to page her.

He hadn't, of course. Too single-minded in his quest he guessed. A weakness he was going to have to overcome.

He was just about to thank him for the suggestion when Ted turned and asked Janelle if she knew Amy's whereabouts. Janelle was much more informative. She not only knew where Amy was, on a job site, but also where she was going to be later.

Not wanting to interrupt her at work, Nick decided to wait until evening when he could catch her in a more casual atmosphere.

And so here he sat, outside the Sundown Lounge, out on the beach. Not his first choice of hangouts, he figured she got used to coming here with Michael, since it was a big beach hangout.

The thought pulled him up short.

She wasn't here with Michael, was she? Trying to patch things up?

He hadn't thought to ask Janelle why she was coming here, he was just so glad to find her he'd hung up as quick as he could, then went to fret and pace over what to wear.

So what if she was with Michael. What was he going to do about it?

He was going to swoop, baby, swoop. But first, he was going to pulverize Michael for the things he'd said about Amy the last time he'd seen him. He'd leave him dangling like the snake he was.

So caught up in his fantasy of revenge, it wasn't until a couple stumbled past him on their way to the beach that he realized he was still sitting in his car.

There was only one way to find out if she was with Michael, and that was to march into that bar.

Too bad he didn't smoke, he thought as he got out of the car. So he would have something to do with his hands. He hadn't been this nervous since he was in high school.

He pushed open the heavy teak door that was carved in

some weird sort of totem pole design. Not sure what that had to do with the beach, he shrugged it off, paid his cover, and walked inside.

The place was…dark. Real dark. There were running lights on the floor, which he guessed delineated cleared areas to walk. Compared to the brightly lit parking lot and neon signs outside, this was midnight on Halloween dark.

He hung back, giving his eyes a chance to adjust before venturing inside, all the while wondering what the heck Amy was doing here.

He passed through the heavy red velvet draperies and into the bar, people beginning to take shape as he maneuvered further into the abyss. Blacklights scattered around the place helped illuminate them by making any white on their clothes glow, so they looked like dismembered ghosts floating through space.

There was an honest-to-goodness lounge singer crooning what he guessed to be some old Dean Martin song.

He really did need to get out more.

Feeling a tug on his shirt he looked down and into the shadowy face of a woman carrying a tray with what looked like test tubes on it.

"Fuzzy navel? Sex on the beach? Vibrating butt plug?" she offered.

Stunned, Nick tilted his head to the side and tried to figure out what to say to such a generous offer. When she nudged her tray at him, he realized she was offering a choice of shooters.

Embarrassed and grateful for the darkness, he declined and moved on.

His vision was getting better and he saw a deejay booth over near the crooner's piano on his left, and on his right a long bar with no stools. Apparently they didn't want you sitting around chatting up the barmaids.

The running lights went up the middle and right along a small dance floor that no one was using. Oh well, he thought. It's early yet. Huge speakers promised to help the deaf to hear the music on deejay nights. But tonight, the place was quiet.

Around the fringes he noted tables, occupied mostly by couples, with a few parties of four mingled throughout. A restroom sign glowed in the distance and using that as a pretense to tour the place and look for Amy, he headed that way.

Once there, he still hadn't found her. Since one of the barmaids watched him, he had no choice but to go into the bathroom.

He made it quick, not wanting to raise suspicion or catch anything. Standing outside the bathroom door, he noticed a small alcove that housed a couple of pay phones. In a bar? He was ready to bet they didn't get used much on deejay night. Who could hear?

Still, it looked like a good place to case the joint from a different angle.

Entering the alcove, he was surprised to see another heavy red drapery, this one not pulled open.

Knowing that Amy wouldn't be in there, but having to check anyway, he nudged it open enough to have a peek.

Nothing so shocking as lap dancing going on. In fact it was just another room with more tables. Still, just the fact that these tables were hidden from the rest of the bar made him suspicious.

Quickly giving it a going over, he spotted the only occupied table. His fingers gripped the fabric so tightly he put a wrinkle in it.

Amy was in here, he could just make out the familiar little bobbing of her ponytail. She wasn't alone, however. She was sitting awfully darn close to someone. Someone big.

Nick squinted, trying to see. From this distance it was impossible to tell for certain, but it didn't look like Michael. Who else could it be? And what should he do about it?

"Outta the way, pal. Me and my honey got a date in that back room."

Startled, Nick swung around to see a tall older woman with extreme hair and a short, bald man. "Sorry, ma'am," he said, moving to the side so they could enter.

"*Aw*, shit. Someone's already back here," she said.

"It's only one couple, Sweetness," her companion said.

"But Punkin," the woman whined. "I wanted a chance for some nooky with you."

The man squirmed, either with pleasure or discomfort, Nick wasn't sure, but he looked up at the ceiling to avoid eye contact with the couple.

"There's always the parking lot," the man coaxed.

"*Oooh*," the woman squealed. "Did you bring the convertible?"

Nick didn't even want to have that vision in his head, so he went to the bar for a drink. Clutching his beer bottle by the neck, he was relieved the couple was gone by the time he got back.

Running his hand through his hair, he checked the room again. Sure enough, Amy and that guy were still in there, seemingly unaware that they had thwarted Sweetness' and Punkin's little tryst.

He couldn't keep standing out here spying on her. He took a quick swig of beer, pulled back the curtain, and swooped in.

Amy looked up, the guy didn't. He thought he saw shock on her face when she recognized him, and he found if he squinted hard enough, it looked like pleasure instead. He wanted to keep squinting, but it was hard to walk with your eyes almost shut, so he opened them wide and headed to her table.

"Nick," Amy gasped, sitting back. "What are you doing here?"

Nick took a second to get used to the sight of her bra glowing through her lightweight shirt like some erotic nightlight. "Hi Amy," he said finally. "Janelle said you'd be here."

"Why would Janelle say I'd be here?" She rested her chin in the palm of her hand while Nick stood next to the table.

He didn't answer, but glanced over at her companion. Amy sat up straight and put her hand out to include him. "Oh, Nick, this is—"

"Dodger Brooks," the man said before Amy could complete the introduction.

"Dodger?" Nick asked, shaking the man's hand and making sure to put a really firm squeeze on it.

"Yeah," he said. "It's a baseball thing. A nickname. You know."

"Yeah," Nick agreed, but he didn't know. He had a football thing, but he didn't go around calling himself Raider, Viking, or Cowboy.

At least, not yet he didn't. That thought didn't sit well. "You here with one of the teams wintering locally?"

"Nah," Dodger said. "Just a fan."

"Have a seat, Nick," Amy said.

He looked around and grabbed a chair from a nearby table. The fit was uncomfortable because the table was so small, but he made sure to scoot as close to Amy as he could, forcing the other guy to move away so she could make room for him.

Crossing his ankle over his knee, he leaned forward to put his beer on the table, then leaned back again, putting his hands behind his head. "So, what are you all doing here tonight?"

"It was Dodger's idea," Amy volunteered. "He says this place has the best Buffalo wings anywhere."

"That right?" Nick asked, looking at Dodger. He wished the light was better so he could stare him down, but for now, he had to make do with just turning his head threateningly.

"Yeah, that's so," Dodger said. "Ever try 'em?"

"Nope, can't say as I have," Nick answered. "Never been here before. How about you, Amy? You ever been here before?"

"No, this is my first time."

Something about the way the other man shifted in his seat when she said that, coupled with her clearly outlined bra area, made him aware that things weren't quite what they seemed where good ol' Dodger was concerned. He'd bet money the pervert brought her here so he could get a tantalizing little peep show without having to explain his actions. "So, you got a wife, Dodger?"

"Nope, like to play the field, if you know what I mean."

Nick nodded his head slowly. He'd bet his best pair of golf shoes that chicken wings weren't all he was looking to get at the Sundown Lounge tonight.

He almost wished Amy was here with Michael; at least she was safe with him. But this guy, well, Nick was increasingly glad he arrived when he did.

He picked up his beer and emptied it, looking at Dodger from beneath his lids as he did. Slapping the beer back down on the table, he turned to Amy. "So, how'd you and ol' Dodger meet?"

"He's a client. We're building a house for him on the beach."

"Really?" Nick wanted to know. "How 'bout that. Was that the site you were visiting all day today?"

Dodger coughed. Good, let the bastard choke while Nick came down on him like some bad-assed big brother.

"Yeah, it's a pretty complicated plan. Lots of little details to be checked out."

"I'll just bet," Nick said. "So, Dodger, what do you do for a living?"

Amy hit him under the table with her fist. The darkness covered his flinch. Frankly, he was enjoying the hell out of this.

"I'm independently wealthy," Dodger said, stuffing a handful of popcorn in his mouth.

"Yeah, lot of that going around in Florida. We're just a short plane hop from Colombia and Mexico. Ever been to Colombia or Mexico, Dodger?" This was more fun than watching a monster truck show from the front row, and almost as muddy.

"Nope, never even been to Texas," Dodger said. "Look, Amy, I think I'll pass on the wings, now that Nick's here to take you home safe and sound. Send your brother out for the next inspection, okay? I want to talk to him about something."

"Oh, but Mr. Brooks," Amy began, but the red velvet curtain was swinging shut behind him. She turned to look at Nick. "You jerk!"

He spread his hands. "Me? What'd I do? I come in and save you from Mr. Backroom Sleezy Nookie King, and I'm a jerk? Amy, he was three kernels of popcorn from calling you Sweetness and offering to take you out to his convertible."

"What in the hell are you talking about?" Amy was so mad she emphasized all the important words for him. "He was my *client*, you big *idiot*! This was a business dinner, you *oaf*."

"Yeah, chicken wings and popcorn. Hell of a meal. Reminds me of the kind my mother used to make." Nick leaned forward to grab the nape of her neck so he could give her a little shake, but she slapped his hand away.

"Look, Nick, for your information, I am twenty-seven years old. I am pretty sure you realized the other day when you were panting over my naked body that I am not a child."

She stood up before continuing, putting on her jacket as she did so. "I can sleep with every damn man on this island if I want to. And how do you know I haven't?"

She stepped around him on her way to the curtain, pausing to chew him out some more. "If I want to strip down to my underwear and dance on tables, it is none of your business. Do you understand?"

Finally finishing what she had to say, she grabbed her purse and stomped to the entrance. Without a backward glance, she left him sitting there with an empty beer bottle and a half a bucket of popcorn.

Wow. She was magnificent! She should give that swooping stuff a try.

Nick thought back to the circling hawk and realized his first attempt at swooping hadn't gone as well as he planned. It lacked a certain…grace.

Twirling the bottle around, he smiled. But he wasn't afraid to try it again.

Too bad it was too dark for him to get a really good look at Dodger. Truth was, Nick doubted he'd recognize him if he saw him in the full light of day. Still, maybe he'd put in a word with his good friend Randy Miller of the local sheriff's office. See if he was interested in Dodger's "independently wealthy" status.

Nick stood up to leave and it was all he could do to keep

from patting himself on the back for being such a fine, upstanding citizen.

* * *

Amy unlocked the car door with one click of her keyless entry. Hopping inside, she was glad she decided to drive her own car, instead of riding with Dodger as he'd suggested. Having her own vehicle gave her a clean getaway, and she didn't want to think about having to hitch a ride with either him or Nick right now.

The car started smoothly and Amy was back out on the two-lane road that ran the length of the small barrier island off the coast of Florida. Coming up on one of the four traffic lights the stretch of land claimed, she turned on her right turn signal and made for home.

It was going to be a long drive. Plenty of time to go over the scene she'd just escaped.

What had Nick been doing? She couldn't figure him out. He'd shown up out of the blue, acting all proprietary, like he owned her or something. And all she'd been trying to do was make good with her client. Her first really big client. The first one she'd been given to handle on her own.

And Nick had ruined it! She was furious.

Oh, she'd been responsible for her own projects before, but they'd been mostly remodels and additions. Never a new construction from the ground up. And never anything this large or challenging. Putting up what amounted to a mansion on the prestigious island was quite a coup. And it was all hers.

Until Nick.

"Damn it," she said, pounding the steering wheel with her fist. She would kill him. That's what she'd do. When he was least expecting it. Maybe some day when he was lounging at

Ted's, she sneak up and stab him in the back like he'd done to her.

No, that wouldn't work. Too many witnesses. Besides, he'd end up making a huge mess all over Janelle's beautiful house, and Amy knew how hard she worked on her home.

All right, she'd invite him over for dinner to her place. Yeah, she'd make all his favorite dishes and each one would be laced with a different kind of poison. A regular deadly smorgasbord. Death by buffet. By the end of the evening she'd be a real Lucrezia whatever that woman's name was.

But how would she get a hold of all the poison she would need without arousing suspicion? This was a mighty small town and if Nick just suddenly keeled over at her house, well, people would ask some really piercing questions. Too bad he was suspicious of her crab dip.

Hmm. She'd have to give this some more thought.

Crossing over the third bridge into town, with only one more to go, she hit upon the perfect plan.

She'd sneak into his house while he was sleeping and smother him. She'd take his pillow, put it over his head, and keep it there until he gave up. If she had to, she'd sit on it. Whatever it took, that's what she'd do. And no one would be the wiser. How would they ever figure out that little ol' her could kill big, strong Nick Granger?

Leaving the last bridge behind and stopping at the red light at Seventy-Fifth Street, she smiled at the idea. Who was she kidding? She wasn't going to kill Nick. If she was perfectly honest with herself, she would just come out and admit that relief had flooded through her when she saw him tonight. She'd just about had a heart attack when Dodger led her to that back room and it was completely empty. He had to go looking for a waitress to take their order, the place was so deserted.

And those creepy blacklights. She shuddered. In her wildest dreams, she never imagined being in a place where you had to touch the other person to make sure they were still there. Of course, this was probably Dodger's plan all along.

A car beeped behind her and she moved through the now green light, halfway to her apartment. Once she got there, she was going to take a nice, long bath. Something she didn't do nearly enough. Now that this day was finally ending, she deserved it.

The rest of the drive passed with her reliving how cute Nick was at the bar, coming to her rescue. She owed him for that one. Big time.

Finally home she heaved a sigh. After her bath, she would make something to eat. She was starving. Popcorn didn't go far and the wings had never arrived. Something else she owed Nick for, since she didn't even like chicken wings.

* * *

Nick pulled into Amy's complex and parked. He assured himself all he wanted to do was apologize for embarrassing her and make sure she was okay. He brushed off the idea that he could call her, because the truth was, he wanted to see her.

She opened the door wearing the same robe she'd worn the day of the spider, only this time her hair hung down her back instead of being confined in a towel. The sense of deja vu gave Nick a twinge of anticipation he quickly squelched.

"Nick," she said, holding the door into her side. "What are you doing here? I can't think of a thing I need to be saved from right now, unless it's the bath I was just getting ready to take."

Thoughts of a naked and wet Amy filled Nick's mind and desire skittered along his nerves. This wasn't going quite as he'd planned, but his ability to plan no longer was the reliable tool it used to be.

"I'm sorry about tonight at the bar," he said, yanking his thoughts back to the present. "I just wanted to make sure you made it home safely."

She raised an eyebrow. "Why wouldn't I? It's not like I haven't lived here my entire life. I know my way around."

She wasn't giving him much room to work, but he was determined to gain back the ground he'd lost. "I know I came on strong back there, and I know Dodger is a client of yours. I know these things in my head, Amy." He paused, leaning one hand on the doorframe. "But in my heart, I know that I care about you too much to leave you alone with men like him. He's not above manipulating situations and people for his own advantage."

Amy nodded. "So, you're telling me you came all the way out to the beach to rescue me from certain unsavory things? What made you decide that I was in danger to begin with? Why did you just show up out of the blue like that?"

Nick squirmed. This wasn't how he wanted to do this, with her in a robe and him checking up on her again. It was too much like returning to the scene of a crime, and when he came totally clean with her, he wanted it to be where they both were comfortable and on an even footing.

He decided to be evasive. "I was looking for something to do tonight, someone to hang out with. All my friends were busy and Ted wasn't interested, so I ended up asking where you were. I thought maybe the two of us could get together."

She stiffened. "Oh, I see. So, as soon as everyone else told you to get lost, you figured maybe good old Amy would be sitting home with nothing to do and she'd be happy, no *grateful* to be your playmate. Is that about the size of it?"

He shook his head, feeling himself sinking deeper. "No, I..."

She didn't let him finish. "So then, when you found out I wasn't home, you went looking for me, figuring you'd just barge in on whatever plans I might have for the evening? Am I getting closer?"

Now he started to get pissed off. All he wanted to do was see her, tell her how he felt, settle some things with her so he could get on with his life. Why was this so hard?

"Because let me tell you something, Mister." She jabbed her finger into his chest. "I don't need your company, I don't need your protection, and I damn sure don't need you checking up on me every time you get an urge to piss somebody off. You got that?"

Oh, he had it all right. Down to his toes, he had it. Now it was her turn to get it. "Now look." He grabbed her hand and held it to his chest while he stared down into her eyes. "I'm real sorry I interrupted your little rendezvous with the poster boy of perverts because he was a client , but I am not going to apologize for caring enough about you to do so." Letting go of her hand, he stepped back. "You've got yourself all twisted up in a knot because you think someone stepped on your precious little toes, but the fact of the matter is, Amy dear, I'd do it again and you can be as mad as you want about it."

Finished with his little tirade, he turned to leave before she started in on him again. He wasn't to the end of the hall before she called his name.

"Yeah?" he said, turning around halfway.

"Thanks." She shut the door.

Nick smiled and headed home. Not exactly the way he

wanted the day to end, but it would have to do.

Chapter Thirteen

There was a Christmas party going on behind him, but instead of partaking of holiday cheer and goodhearted wishes, Nick was keeping one eye on the front door and the other eye on his watch. "When is she going to get here?"

Unbelievable. Nick ran his fingers through his hair. He was stalking his best friend's sister.

Even so, he had to get this off his chest, had to tell her how he felt. This seemed like as good a place as any. Besides, he was out of time. The team was putting pressure on him, expecting him to show up in a couple of days. The time to lay himself bare was now. And if Amy didn't feel the same way he did, or if she was unwilling to find out, well he'd hop on the plane and move on with his life. But he had to know. The limbo of one-sided love was killing him.

That was the plan, anyway. He wasn't sure if he could pull it off, but he was going to try.

At last the door opened and a blast of December air rushed in. An arctic cold front had come through the day before, bringing wintry weather just in time for the holidays.

Nick smiled with relief. "Finally!"

He went to meet her, knocking over a potted palm in his haste. "What took you so long? You're the last one to get here," he said, standing the poor palm upright. Yessir. It was a good thing he didn't have to worry about making a positive first impression.

She looked up at him and grinned, graciously not laughing at his clumsiness, then rose up on her toes to kiss his cheek. Nick's heart skipped a beat and then pounded to catch up. Man, he hoped tonight went as planned or he was going to have to do something drastic. He wasn't sure what, he hadn't planned that far ahead.

"Did you forget where your brother lived?" Now that she was safely out of his reach and he could think again, he was a little annoyed that chitchat was the best he could come up with for conversation. He had plans to bare his soul, and he was settling for inanities?

"Why? Did you miss me? Couldn't find anyone else to annoy?" Her tone was teasing and he breathed a sigh of relief that she wasn't holding his recent behavior against him.

"As a matter of fact, I did. Miss you, that is." He put his arm around her shoulders in brotherly fashion and tried not to mind the effort it cost him to do so. "Take a walk with me, Amy. I've got something I need to tell you."

Her face showed concern, but she wasn't giving in to it. "A walk?" she asked. "I just got here. What's so important you can't tell me here?" She turned from his casual embrace and faced him. "Is this about your job transfer? Because if it is, Ted already told me. We're both going to miss you. I can't believe you can't stay until after Christmas."

That's it? She would miss him? Like her brother would miss him? Nick took that blow like a man. He pretended it was nothing.

However, he couldn't pretend that this was going as planned. Not that he'd had much of a plan. What he'd really had was some vague vision of the two of them strolling along on a cloudless, starry night, snuggling together for warmth. He'd state his case in a couple of sentences and she'd throw herself into his arms, confessing that she'd always loved him too.

Reality hit him just a second before panic did.

It was definitely time for something drastic. He took her hand in his and opened his mouth to tell her what had been secret for so long.

"Hey, come on you guys," a voice intruded. "It's time to go caroling." Ted led the party their way. "Hi Amy. It's about time you got here. Now get your coat back on."

Amy kissed his cheek exactly as she'd kissed Nick's cheek earlier.

Everyone crowded into the foyer, hunting for their winter coats and arguing over whether it was more Christmas-y to go dashing through the snow in a one-horse open sleigh, or to stay home roasting chestnuts on an open fire. Nick wished they'd all decide *Silent Night* was the way to go, but he wasn't getting his wishes tonight.

He'd have to try again some other time. Maybe New Year's Eve. Or maybe he'd make it his New Year's resolution. Or maybe he'd just catch a leprechaun and make him do his bidding come St. Patrick's Day.

But he wouldn't be here for any of those things. He'd be off in the Midwest, taking care of cheerleaders and pretending he worked for the NFL.

"You guys go on ahead, we'll catch up."

Amy stared at him, her brows forming a concerned *V*.

Finally they all went out the door, laughing and having a much better time than Nick was.

"What's wrong, Nick?" Amy asked.

Everything, he thought. "Nothing," he said.

"You're not having second thoughts, are you?"

No, he most certainly was not.

He knew she referred to his job, but he was thinking only about her. But he needed the right words, the right moment, to tell her how he felt.

Ready to give up, he said, "Looks like we'll be taking that walk after all." He picked up her heavy coat and bundled her inside, then shrugged into his own. He opened the door and ushered her outside onto the porch, determined to end this lame attempt at winning her.

What was he thinking? He couldn't leave. He'd quit the stupid job before he even started it and stay here.

The idea astounded him. He'd waited his whole life for this opportunity, promised to take whatever position they offered him. Willing to work his way up to prove his loyalty. He'd sent out resumes every six months for one-third of his life, to prove himself.

And for what? To turn tail now and chuck it? To say "Sorry, guys. I was just kidding."

Damn straight. He'd turned that organization into his whole life. And his whole life had been about being safely uninvolved. It had given him something to strive for, to take his mind off the one thing he really wanted but feared he couldn't have.

Amy. He looked at her now and his spirits soared. He knew what he wanted. Knew with a clarity that matched the winter air. He was in for the long haul and he was going to throw himself into the impossible. He was going to pursue her until she either gave in and loved him, or...

He wouldn't consider the alternative. He was in this to win.

A positive outlook was a wonderful thing, he decided as he shut the door behind him.

Facing him on the porch she looked up and beyond him, a smile of mischief on her face. Before he could look up to see what was so amusing she grabbed his jacket by the front and pulled him to her, planting her lips directly on his. His arms went around her and when she would've pulled away, he held her still.

He was drowning and he just didn't care as long as he could drown with her in his arms. His heart pounded and blood raced through his veins. Everything in him had been waiting for this moment.

She released him far too soon and unable to think what he should do next, Nick did the only thing he could think of.

"Amy, I love you." He froze. Oh, that was smooth, and totally unexpected. He'd meant to end this night and regroup to try again later, not blurt it out like that. Heck, if he couldn't win her by knocking over a defenseless plant, what made him think shocking her would do it?

"What did you say?" she asked, a look of either disbelief or joy on her face, he couldn't tell which in the dim porch light.

Like it or not, this was the moment he'd been given. "I said, Amy, I love you." Man, it felt great to finally say that out loud.

There was more he was going to say. Now that he'd started, he wanted to make sure his case was laid out all neat and tidy, but she interrupted him.

"Finally!" She echoed his earlier greeting to her. "What took you so long?"

He didn't have an answer for that. He was too busy coping with the rush of hope that came out of nowhere.

Fortunately Amy wasn't waiting for him to explain himself. "Nick, I'm not the one you had to convince. I've been waiting for you to realize this for years." She pointed above his head and wiggled her eyebrows suggestively.

He glanced up and spotted the mistletoe dangling suggestively over his head. Thank God Ted was weird enough to hang mistletoe on the front porch.

Slowly, deliberately, in keeping with his personality and the seriousness of the moment, Nick lowered his head and kissed her. Gently, then with growing insistence.

Even without her willingness he doubted he'd be able to keep from gathering her closer, nearer to his heart.

She molded herself to him and everything suddenly made sense. There'd be no more searching or longing or proving himself. He had all that within arm's reach and he was going to make sure that's where she stayed.

Forever.

Epilogue

Amy dawdled around the hotel bathroom, brushing her hair and fluffing the negligee around her. She'd already brushed her teeth, *twice*, so there really wasn't any reason for her to linger here. And still she did.

Holding her left hand up to the light she smiled at the twinkling diamond. She and Nick were married. She could hardly believe it, but it was true. Ever since this afternoon and a four-hour plane flight, it had been so.

"Hey, Mrs. Granger." Nick knocked on the door. "Are you ever coming out here?"

A thrill shot through her hearing her new name. "Just a second, okay? I'm still not ready."

"Well, baby, I'm ready enough for both of us."

His husky promise made her quiver. She wished she wasn't so nervous, but she was terrified of disappointing him. And yet, even afraid, she was aware of the ache his words evoked in her. Low in her belly and expanding, the feeling never left her when he was around.

Having known each other forever they decided not to wait long to get married, and so their short engagement had been taken up with wedding plans. There was no time for intimacy. Not the kind Amy wanted, anyway.

Nick wasn't much help, claiming since they'd waited this long, what was a few more weeks? Now, here they were, married. Finally. Amy was dying for him, but she couldn't work up the courage to leave the bathroom.

Which was too ridiculous for words. This was her wedding night, not some childish game of hide and seek.

But the truth was, she hadn't been exactly honest with Nick. She hadn't been precisely dishonest, either. More like the question had never come up, and she'd never made an issue of it. Had never thought to. She figured it would be a nice little surprise for the wedding night.

Only now, she wasn't sure it wouldn't turn out to be more of a mistake than a surprise.

Then she remembered how he'd given up the football job and decided to stay in their hometown, claiming he didn't want to leave anymore than she did. It had just taken him a few decades longer than her to realize it.

Chanting to herself that of course Nick loved her, and he was hers forever now, she raised her chin and opened the door.

Nick's jaw dropped and her courage soared.

"You are gorgeous."

"So are you," she said, admiring him as well.

Going into his arms, she raised her head for a kiss, but he swung her into his arms instead, depositing her on the bed.

Panic made her wary and she moved to the other side. Seeing his look of confusion, she patted the side of the bed next to her, implying she'd moved over to make room.

With a wolfish grin, he took her up on her offer. He pulled her into his arms and rolled her under him. After a brief kiss, Amy pushed him back slightly.

"Nick, I need to tell you something," she said into his chest.

"Can't it wait?" he wanted to know. "Because I'm not sure how much longer I can."

"Well, it's about…that." She glanced up at him. "About making love," she explained, seeing his confusion.

"What about it? You want me to wear a condom?" The crestfallen look on his face would've been funny if she weren't so nervous.

"No!" she said. "I'm not worried about getting pregnant. I think having your baby would be a wonderful thing. It's just…"

He leaned back and stared into her eyes, concern etched on his face. "Amy?" he said. "What's wrong? You haven't changed your mind, have you?"

It was a ridiculous thing to say after she'd just admitted to wanting his baby, but Amy didn't notice. "No, I haven't changed my mind. But, there's something you don't know about me."

He stiffened. "What could I possibly not know about you? And why would it make any difference to me?"

She'd come too far to go back now, she realized. Looking into his worried eyes, she knew no matter what she said, it wouldn't matter to him. Warming to her tale, she rubbed her hand up and down his chest. "It's something kinda radical in this day and age. Something shocking, even."

He reciprocated by trailing his fingers over her breasts. "Yes, go on."

"The fact is, Nick," she paused for effect, "this is my first time. Not just with you. Ever." She waited.

He froze in disbelief, and then as her words washed over him, joy spread across his face. "What about you and Michael," he said, stunned. "I thought for sure you and he…"

"Nope, never," she said with a smile.

"Good, cuz I gotta tell you. I really hate that guy." He took a deep breath and let it out. "I can't believe it."

"Well, you can believe it," she reassured him. "Is that okay with you?"

"Okay? Are you kidding? I thought this day was the best day of my life just because you were finally mine. Then I find out I don't have to wear a condom, you never slept with that loser, Michael, and you waited for me." He took her face in his hands and planted a kiss that would rock the foundation of a building. "Sweetheart, you couldn't tell me anything that would top this."

"I love you," she said simply.

"Except that."

Gerrie Shepard

Coming
Christmas 2004
From Echelon Press

A Home for Christmas

By

Deborah Grace-Staley

Book Two

In the

Angel Ridge Series

Chapter One

They say you can never go home.

Janice Thornton glided up to the curb in front of the old two-story Victorian and killed the engine. It looked much the same; gingerbread trim eaves, wide wraparound porch with wicker furniture. The house was huge, but it had always felt cozy to her. Sitting here looking at it through adult eyes, she realized the appeal had never been the house itself, but the home her grandparents had made here. Their house had been her ideal of what a home should be. A home she'd longed for as a young child. A home she'd never had with her own parents.

Janice slid her sunglasses off and laid them in the empty passenger seat next to her. She always got sentimental around the holidays. She didn't know why. Her formative years had been spent at exclusive boarding schools. Christmases always involved a trip, either with her parents, or more often, with school friends. Each year, her grandmother had invited her to spend Christmas break in Angel Ridge, but her mother wouldn't hear of such a thing. She'd always been embarrassed by her humble roots and didn't want her daughter revisiting them.

Janice hadn't been in Angel Ridge, Tennessee since just before her grandmother's funeral some ten years ago. It hadn't changed much. Tall, old houses lined one side of a street that ran high above the Little Tennessee River, with a church steeple just visible a few blocks over. It was a sleepy little town that time seemed to have forgotten, but for some reason, it burned in Janice's memory like a warm, inviting fire on a cold winter morning.

When she looked back at the old Victorian, she noticed that a man had appeared from behind the house carrying a ladder. Upon further investigation, she noted the pile of Christmas lights that lay on the ground in the front yard. Janice smiled. She was glad to see that this man, whoever he was, continued her grandfather's tradition of decking the house out in grand style for Christmas.

The man leaned the ladder against the house. Next, he turned toward a mound of lights. He looked at her then and smiled. Her breath caught and hung inside her chest. It was an easy smile, full of good humor that enticed a person to come sit a spell on the porch and enjoy the unseasonably warm, late autumn sunshine.

He was tall and lean with whipcord muscles. He wore faded and well-worn jeans with a T-shirt that looked like it had once been black, but now was more a soft charcoal dotted with paint stains. A tan leather tool belt slung low across his narrow hips. A lock of thick, dark hair fell across his tanned forehead as he bent to retrieve the lights.

Janice shifted and the leather seat creaked. She cracked the window a bit as she felt a sheen of sweat mist her forehead.

She wondered what he must be thinking, but he acted as if seeing a strange woman in a new silver BMW parked outside his home was an every Saturday morning occurrence. He turned, and without giving her a second glance, started up the ladder. He stopped about eight rungs up and leaned to his right, toward one of the bay windows on the ground floor.

Shifting the lights to his other hand, he reached out to pull at something above the window. He teetered. One foot went up in the air as he tried to shift back to find his balance. But the ladder tipped sideways with the movement, and Janice watched in disbelief as he began to fall.

Years of medical school, emergency room rotations, residency, and private practice had honed her instincts so that she didn't even give it a conscious thought. She was out of her car and at his side almost before he hit the boxwoods and rolled to the ground.

"Oh, jeez," he groaned.

Janice had already clicked into professional mode. "Don't worry, I'm a doctor. Try not to move." She ran her hands down his arms, checking for broken bones. "Where does it hurt?"

The man chuckled. It was a low rumble that had a crazy effect on her. And that smile…it should be registered as a lethal weapon.

"If I said everywhere, would you keep doing that?"

Her hands froze on his hard, muscled thigh. *Get a grip*, she told herself. The man had fallen at least ten feet. He needed to be checked out. Thoroughly. She gave him what she hoped was a look that conveyed that this was a serious matter and continued down his leg. Firm muscles contracted and bunched beneath the soft, nearly threadbare denim.

Janice cleared her throat and tried to speak around the knot that had formed there. "That was quite a fall. Does anything feel broken? Strained? Any pain at all?"

The man tried to sit up, but she restrained him with a firm hand at his shoulder. "You really shouldn't move."

"Dr., um…"

"Thornton. Janice Thornton."

"Dr. Thornton, I'm fine. Really," he insisted, grabbing her hand as she began checking his other leg. "I'd have to fall further than that to hurt anything other than my pride."

Janice frowned. She was almost completely distracted by the crinkles at the corners of his eyes that said a smile came easy to him, but she knew that often one could have injuries that didn't present with pain after a fall like that. She turned her attention to his head. "You could have a concussion."

She sank her fingers into his thick, dark hair at the place where an almost indiscernible sprinkling of gray fanned out from his temples. His scalp felt warm, and her fingers tingled as she checked for knots. She faltered when she looked into his eyes. Fringed by incredibly long, inky eyelashes, they were a striking silvery blue that stood out against the framing of his dark hair and skin. He'd propped himself up on one elbow so that his torso almost touched hers. She stopped breathing when she felt his breath, warm and enticing against her cheek.

He reached to touch her face, but Janice sat back on her heels. "There doesn't seem to be any knots. No bruising or contusions." She couldn't stop herself from reaching out to remove a sprig of rich, green boxwood leaves from his hair. "Um, what about your neck? Does it hurt?"

Before he could answer, she slid her fingers around to the back of his neck and grasped his chin with her free hand. He had a strong jaw. She'd always been a sucker for guys with strong jaws. "Gently," she whispered, as she turned his head from one side to the other. "Any pain?" She felt a sensual web forming around them, powerless to extricate herself from its seductive weave. Janice watched in fascination as the Adam's apple bobbed in the tanned column of his throat.

Embrace the Passion with an
Echelon Embrace

Ain't Love Grand
ISBN 1-59080-298-5

Dana Taylor
$10.99

Second Chance at Forever
ISBN 1-59080-005-2

Natalie Damschroder
$12.99

Zorroc
ISBN 1-59080-318-3

Lil Gibson
$13.99

A Brush With Love
ISBN 1-59080-266-7

Jo Barrett
$11.99

House of Cards
ISBN 1-59080-187-3

Blair Wing
$10.99

Wild Montana Hearts
ISBN 1-59080-127-X

Sarah Storme
$11.99

Dark Shines My Love
ISBN 1-59080-252-7

Alexis Hart
$10.99

Caribbean Charade
ISBN 1-59080-209-8

Louise Perry
$11.99

When Opportunity Knocks
ISBN 1-59080-293-4

T.A. Ridgell
$14.49

Raphaela's Gift
ISBN 1-59080-277-2

Sydney Laine Allan
$13.99

To order visit
www.echelonpress.com
Or visit your local
Retail bookseller

Meet the author:

Gerrie Shepard was born on Superbowl Sunday. Okay, that's not true, but she's had birthdays preempted because of the Superbowl off and on practically her whole life. The good side of this is that she's not technically as old as she should be.

Certainly not old enough to have four children, ranging in age from college to elementary school, or married for almost twenty years. And impossible that she's been reading romance novels for twenty-five years.

As cliché as it sounds, Ms. Shepard got started writing the old fashioned way. She read a couple of books that made her think, "I can do this." After all, hadn't English teachers through the years declared her book reports to be shining examples to the rest of the student body? So, at the age of eleven, she got busy on a gothic novel involving gargoyles, magic jewels, and a heroine named Margaret, discovering quickly that writing was hard! Really hard! She promptly put it off for almost thirty years before realizing she should give it another try.

Happily (joyfully!) her first novel sold to Echelon Press. This means that she has to get busy on another one (which proves that writing is still really hard, but worth it)! When she's not writing Ms. Shepard is gardening, riding horses, or reading, reading, reading.

Printed in the United States
22085LVS00001B/27